# Mayday!

## TINDER LOVE IN THE GOLDEN YEARS.

# KAT ADDAMS

*"I think it's your mental attitude. So many of us start dreading age in high school, and that's a waste of a lovely life. 'Oh ... I'm thirty, oh, I'm forty, oh, fifty.' Make the most of it."*

—Betty White

# One

## MARILYN

*I* rolled myself out of bed, stretching and making noises that I hadn't made since that time twelve years ago with Brother Anthony from church. I'd said more hallelujahs that night with him than I had all year in the pulpit.

Forgive me, Father, but that man had had me from the moment he lowered his eyes and whispered, "Good morning, Ms. May. Pleased to see you at service, Ms. May."

My name rolled off his tongue like oil in a frying pan—sizzling hot. The devilish grin he proudly wore should have warned me, but instead, it only made things worse. I'd not been able to get home fast enough to serve him some of my famous sweet tea—and by sweet tea, I meant, the banging sixty-four-year-old body of mine.

But, of course, that had been twelve years ago, and I was seventy-six now. There'd been much less sagging and dragging going on, and I'd still not had to buy adult diapers. Wasn't that some shit? No one told you when you got old and cranky, you also started piddlin' when you sneezed, hiccuped, farted, or coughed. No, there were lots of things my mom had never told me about aging. Truth be told, if she had ever passed on this depressing wisdom, I wouldn't have listened anyway. I had wanted to be a cool mom and a cool grandma. And being cool didn't include wearing diapers and soaking dentures.

I groaned as I pushed my heels into the cold wooden floorboards of my chilly room. I pushed myself off the bed, falling back, one, two, four times before I got my footing. No one told you that either. Balance and strength weren't something that stuck around in old age. It was only yesterday that I'd come so damn close to breaking my hip and being laid up in the hospital for who knew how long.

I'd been at my nosy neighbor, Gloria's, house, listening to the latest neighborhood gossip. I didn't particularly like Gloria. She and I'd had some drama way back. But these lonely days called for some type of human connection, so I'd brought over some cookies and listened to her drone on and on about the other old coots down the street. When her doorbell rang right in the middle of a dramatic tale, I jumped up so high that I fell off her musty, checkered couch. Thankfully, I'd had enough sense to put my palms down and ease my fall. I guessed I still had my reflexes.

I shuffled my feet across the floor, shivering all the way to the iron radiator to kick it with my slipper. This damn thing had been broken for two years. It only worked when it wanted to, and usually, that was after I'd given it a good whack with a brush, a book, a frying pan, or anything within my reach. It would turn on for a little while, but it always seemed to putter out not long after it had gotten going— just like a man. That was why I'd named my radiator Roger. It wasn't exactly my idea to call him Roger. It was my friend Grayson's idea.

Grayson and his boyfriend, John, had come over to take a look at it last winter. John was pretty handy, but Grayson wouldn't know what a wrench looked like if I hit him upside the head with it. Those two teetered about with the furnace, making clanging noises and inspecting every inch. But in the end, they'd declared that they had no idea what the issue was and named it after an ex-boyfriend of Grayson's who had the same characteristics—quick to turn on but hadn't lasted long at all and annoyingly frustrating. Hence, my furnace was now Roger.

Roger had been a good man back in the day when I was married and popping out babies like every other Southern woman I knew in these parts. But when I had gotten rid of my no-good husband over twenty years ago, things had started to get tough around here. I'd had to learn to do a lot on my own, and I had been okay with that then. But at seventy-six, I was not. I needed a man to fix my heater, to cut my grass, and to grill me a steak that I could hardly chew because, once again, no one told you that your teeth would go soft and fall out when you were old.

As much as the thought of putting up with another Roger pained me, I decided to give it one last shot. If I could have some old fart in my back pocket to play Mr. Fix It and all I had to do was bat my eyes and serve him some sweet tea—the real stuff—I could do it. Never mind having him leave his dentures on my nightstand overnight or reminding him to take his Viagra. That ship had sailed for me a long time ago.

Like I always told my friend Klara, "If you don't use it, it shrivels up."

I didn't look down below much these days, but if I did, I was sure I'd see a wrinkled old raisin.

I poured myself a cup of hot coffee and sat in front of the TV. Klara was supposed to be coming by this morning. Every Monday, she'd come by my house and check on me, usually bringing doughnuts and playing catch-up on her weekends. I didn't mind it. I needed the company. After my daughter had moved to Outer Forks, I rarely had guests anymore. Sunday supper with my family had become few and far between, but between Grayson and John, and Klara and her new husband, Chris, I was more than happy. Any more people than that, and I might just end up stroking out—or at least pretending to. I could only handle so much.

It was only the nights that had been getting hard to swallow. Again, that must be something to do with old age. I'd never been bothered by being alone. But lately, my bed was feeling mighty cold at night. Probably because that dumbass Roger wasn't warming it properly.

My mind went back to Brother Anthony from church. We had kept up our fling all during the summer months, but we had known it couldn't last. He was a traveling preacher, and he had been called to another church for a permanent job, sixteen hours away. He knew how to work me, but ain't no man worth me traveling that far to keep him as mine. I'd let him slap my ass one last time, and then I'd kicked his butt on out of here.

I sat back on my lumpy couch and smiled to myself, remembering that Brother Anthony and I were part of the reason this couch was so worn out. I took a long sip of my coffee as I heard Klara's car door slam. I groaned, forgetting that I hadn't unlocked the door so I would need to get up again. I set my mug down on the table and pushed myself to my heels three times before getting to my feet.

"Good morning, sunshine," I said, pursing my lips and opening the door.

"Bringing you your Monday rays of golden sun and doughnuts to start your week off right!" Klara bounced through my doorstep and set the doughnuts on the table before going into the kitchen and coming back with her own cup of coffee.

I hadn't even made it back to the couch yet before she settled into her spot next to me.

"Make yourself at home, dear." I rolled my eyes.

"Thanks. I am. Except it's colder than a witch's titty in here, Ms. May! Is Roger acting up again?" Klara sank back into the cushions.

"Yep! Just like a man. Good-for-nothing men, good-for-nothing heater. Although—and ever tease me about this, I'll cut you—I have been thinking about finding a man to fix the place up around here." I eased myself back down onto the couch and reached for a doughnut.

"You don't need a man for that! It's the year 2020! There are all sorts of women who know how to fix stuff up, myself included. You tell me what you need, and I'll put on my tool belt and fix it."

"No offense, child, but I need someone who doesn't have a new husband and a life. I know how all that goes. I've been there, done that, and I'm not going to be the crotchety old lady interfering in y'all's time. If I had an old lady butting her miserable life into mine anytime I got my panties down for my new, sexy husband, I'd have to ship her off to a nursing home."

"Well, no offense to you, too, but you already are the crotchety old lady. You haven't interfered in anything though. You know Chris and I love you. I'm not sure why, but we do." Klara set her mug down and turned toward me.

She and I could argue all day and still be friends that night. Banter was our love language.

"Don't go getting all soft on me. Put that mug back in your hands and carry on. We are here to discuss your weekend and your next big novel, which you said you're basing on me this time, right?"

"Expert subject-changer. Hmm ..." She tapped her chin. "I need some inspiration. You could play a role in that department now that I think about it." She grabbed her mug again and took a long sip.

"Oh, yeah? You writing about a superwoman then? I didn't know you wrote fantasy, but I'll be your role model, sure." I licked the doughnut glaze off my sticky fingers, smacking my lips and smirking.

Klara had already dedicated one of her novels to me, but I'd yet to make my debut in one. At least, to my knowledge. I'd combed through her books, looking for any resemblance to me, but the closest I'd gotten was to a mentally deranged homeless woman named Frieda.

"A love story! You know that. You said you're looking for a man. Why not look for one to do more than fix your house up? Why not look for one to knock your full-coverage stockings off too?"

Klara stared at me over her steaming mug. I couldn't see her lips, but I was sure they twitched in an attempt to hold back a laugh.

"You'll be here, too, one day, Ms. Famous Author. Don't you think your money is going to buy you time. You'll be wearing adult diapers and taking Geritol in the blink of an eye. Better pop them babies out beforehand, or your eggs are gonna dry up. I keep on telling you, but you don't—"

"You're still doing it," she muttered, setting her coffee back down.

"Doing what?"

"Changing the subject. You went back to me. We are talking about you. I said you could be my inspiration for my next novel. Maybe I could write about love through the older years? What do you think? Since you tell me that no one tells you blah, blah, blah about aging, you can tell me. Tell me everything and also tell me how your love life works."

"I ain't got a love life. I can tell you how everything works and, most importantly, doesn't work, but as far as a man … I only have that dumbass Roger in there." I nodded my head in the direction of my failure of a radiator.

"How about we find you a man to fix your home up, Roger included, while also finding me some new inspo for my novel? I'll help you. We can work as a team."

"Lord, Klara, you've got too much time on your hands." I shook my head, waving her off with my hand.

"And so do you! What do you even have planned today? Watching *Wheel of Fortune* and grumbling about people speeding down your street?"

*Crap. She's right.*

"I watch *Family Feud*. That white girl turning those letters on the other show gets my nerves in a tizzy. I can't stand to watch her. She's too smiley for me. And people do drive crazy down here! What if I'm hobbling out there to check my mail, and some turd nugget comes flying out from nowhere and hits me? You know I have to use a walker to get down my drive now? Damn long driveway. Would have moved to a retirement facility if they didn't cost an arm and a leg," I grumbled.

"Still changing the subject. Wow. All right, Ms. May, do you want your stuff fixed or not? We can treat it like a game if you want."

"I wouldn't even know where to start! Church?" I felt the corners of my mouth spread as I thought about Brother Anthony. Maybe this wasn't going to be a bad idea after all.

"You could. Although, these days, we use apps. Can I see your phone? I'll get it, just tell me where it is." She rose to her feet.

"Over there on the kitchen counter. What do you need it for? What kind of app? I don't know how to do anything on those damn smart-things, except text and make a phone call. Grandbabies tried teaching me, but it's over my head."

Klara took the few steps to the kitchen and hurried back with my phone, scooting herself close to me. "Now, look, I'm going to download an app. It's like a program. It is going to find you a man."

"How the hell?" I started.

"Just wait and watch. Listen for a minute. I know you have a hard time keeping that big mouth of yours shut, but just hear me out. I'm downloading Tinder for you. You set your distance range and age range, and you're good to go. We'll plug in your stats, and you can get to swiping." Her fingers flew over my phone, arranging this and that and I didn't know what else. "Oh, super important. Do you have a good picture of you?"

"From ten years ago. Why?" I watched her as she typed in a maximum of a hundred-plus on an age range. "One hundred? They ain't going to be able to fix a damn thing, except for their life insurance policy—over their landline—when they see what I'm bringing to the table!"

"I like that spirit of yours. You need that in online dating. Good for you. I doubt you'll get hit on by many men over a hundred. I think they usually die around eighty. I set your minimum to thirty, so maybe you can play cougar. Here, let me take a picture of you for your profile. You can't put a ten-year-old photo up. I mean, some people do, but we won't play that game. We want real, authentic people. For you and my book." She stood up, smoothing down my hair.

"What are you doing?" I batted her hands away.

"You can't put yourself out there, looking like you just rolled out of bed!"

"But I did just roll out of bed!" I groaned. "Go get some damn lipstick out of my bathroom and whatever else, and let's do this. I'm already ready to go back to bed." Yet another one of those great things that happened when you were getting old—no energy.

She quickly ran out of the room and back, carrying a fistful of makeup that I'd had stuck in a drawer ever since my divorce. "Sit still and let me get this on you." She tilted my chin to the side, observing my face. "Ms. May, you don't have any wrinkles. Do you Botox?"

"No, baby. Black don't crack. You ain't never noticed that?"

"Huh. No, but I guess you're right. Lucky lady—and an even luckier man who is going to date you." She bounced on her heels as she put more makeup on me than I'd even put on myself when I was young and wild—too wild.

"Are you almost done?" I said through parted lips as she swiped a skanky shade of red over them. I'd had that color since my early twenties. I curled my lips back at the stale, crumbled texture that was somehow disgusting and oddly satisfying at the same time. It tasted like the flavor of reckless behavior from long ago.

"Done. Now, tilt your head to the left and raise your chin." Klara stepped back, holding up my phone and snapping picture after picture. "Perfect! Now, let me go through, find a good one, slap a filter on it, and post it."

"I have no idea what you're doing, but this'd better make me rich and famous." I slumped in my seat and reached for another doughnut.

"Not making any promises, but here, that's your profile." She handed me my phone. "Now, all you have to do is swipe left past any men you don't think you'd want as a friend or lover or fix-it man—whatever. If you do see someone you're interested in, you swipe right. If that person swiped right on you, then Tinder will see it as a match. Then, you two can send messages to each other. Easy-peasy. Any questions?"

"Do I get a cut of royalties for this?" I muttered, staring down at a photo of a forty-six-year-old man in a public restroom, flipping off the camera.

"Oh, Ms. May, you know I'll always take care of you. I have to run though. I only had a minute today. Chris is coming back from a lecture, and I want to make the house nice. Damn cats have been tearing up everything! Now, get to swiping! I'll be back next week for a report! Take notes if you have to! Oh, and don't meet any yet! They could be serial killers. I'll help you figure all that out. Just find some good ones, flirt a little, get to know them." She walked over to the kitchen, putting her mug in the dishwasher.

"I don't even remember agreeing to this," I sighed. "You are going to give me another heart attack."

She turned to Roger and reared her foot back, letting it go into a ninja kick to his side. He immediately fired up. "No, I'm just trying to help. Maybe get that old heart of yours working again along with this damn piece-of-crap furnace."

"Thank you, Klara. Don't know what I'd do without you and the gang." I set my phone down, trying to pull myself up to see her out.

"Now, don't *you* go getting soft on *me*. Don't get up. I'll lock the door. See you soon!" She waved her hand, smiling before she left with her signature pep in her step.

I guessed if anything were to come out of this, at least it made her happy. And that girl was like a daughter to me these days. She took care of me. I picked up my phone and began to swipe in the name of research, Klara, and maybe even in hopes of kicking Roger to the curb for a newer model.

# *Two*

## CLYDE

*I* snored myself awake again. This was the third night I'd fallen asleep in my recliner in front of the TV. I'd tried to stay up late to watch the night shows, but more often than not lately, I ended up rudely awoken by those loud infomercials. I swore they turned the volume up on those commercials just to get old people like me to listen. Course, they must think we were all hard of hearing. I was not.

My seventy-eight-year-old body was still going as strong as a horse. That was me—*Clyde*sdale. At least, that was the nickname I'd received years ago when I checked into this godforsaken place. It wasn't my idea to live in a retirement community, but my children forced me in here not long after my wife, Katherine, had passed away. She was a good one. Kept me fed so much that I had to walk around with the top button of my pants undone all the time. Her biscuits and gravy made me want to smack her ass good and tell her, "Good job, woman." But she didn't like that.

No, my poor wife was a bit of a Goody Two-shoes. Our sex life had kicked the bucket as soon as she popped out all those kids she'd begged me for. After our children were born, we had sex on anniversaries, Valentine's Day, Father's Day, and October 5th. No reason or holiday in October, but I insisted on getting laid that day every year because it was a normal day, and damn it, I deserved my wife's hot piece of ass on a regular ol' day. I'd counted down the days to October 5th every year.

And now, being a single man in a retirement community, I was the most eligible bachelor in here. These residents' husbands were dropping left and right. But me? I was Clydesdale. Nothing was knocking me out.

The key to a long life was exercise, crossword puzzles, a multivitamin, and bran cereal every morning to get my insides working. It never failed. My body might be sagging and dragging just a bit these days, but I sure didn't have a potbelly anymore. Not since my wife had passed anyway. I'd grieved for a good long while on that, but then I'd gotten my life together and gone on the prowl. Getting into shape hadn't been too difficult for someone who never learned to cook. Beans and toast, hot dogs in the microwave, and a bowl of cereal were all I cared to make. I didn't have time to go fooling around in no kitchen. I had man shit to do. Like woo the new grandma in apartment 523.

I'd had more sex in just the last few years than I'd had my entire life. These ladies in here were hungry. They didn't call this place Knotty Pines for nothing. I never met women any naughtier than these old bitties. As soon as I'd stepped through the doors of this geriatric college dorm, I'd had them wheeling their wheelchairs up to me to take a closer look. Poor Ms. Wilson had hobbled so quickly down the hall with her walker, she had fallen and fractured a hip. Talk about making an entrance.

But lately, things had been quiet. I'd not had a woman in eight or so months. All of them were the same old, sad tale, and to be honest, it was depressing. I didn't like to think of myself as an old man. I still had vitality. I liked to walk, run, lift weights, be active. I was a silver fox—both on top of my head and down below. Scratch that. I was a *platinum* fox. I had a lot to offer, and these ladies around here didn't. Most I noticed went downhill fast as soon as they moved in. And even worse, they didn't offer me much over a warm bed. I wanted more these days—a warm meal, a warm bed, good conversation.

It was a sad existence for most people here. They had no family, no love, no anyone. Take that all away from someone, and the only thing they had to look forward to was bingo night, whatever they could call the sex they still tried to do these days, and hopefully going out of this world peacefully in their sleep. I hated to sound morbid, but it was the truth. That was why I was finished with the women of Knotty Pines.

I had recently expanded my horizons and jumped into the online dating world, courtesy of an app called Tinder that my great-grandson had come by to install.

If they'd had these things when I was growing up, life would have been much easier. Instead, I remembered combing through the newspaper ad personals. That was a terrible idea for dating. You never knew what you'd get. One day, you might meet up and date a gorgeous movie-star actress, and the next, you could be dining with a beaver. And not the between-her-legs kind of beaver. I was talking about a woman with teeth she could scratch her chin with and a hairy forehead to boot. Newspaper personals were the Russian roulette of the dating world. But with Tinder, if I didn't think they'd get my heart pumping, I could just swipe them to the left without breaking any hearts.

So far, I'd swiped through the entire city of Memphis—twice—for women my age and admittedly quite younger. You never knew who might have a daddy—or in my case, a granddaddy—kink. As I'd said, I was a platinum Clydesdale. I'd been deprived of sexual relations for a very long time, and I didn't have much time left on this here earth to make up for it. If I could find a respectable lady in the streets and a freak in the sheets to be a companion for the rest of my years, I'd die a happy, old man.

I wiped a string of drool from my open mouth and cleared my dry throat. I never used to snore, but this winter had gotten my sinuses so messed up that I swore all that stuffiness was somehow making my nose hairs grow. Last time I'd looked at myself in the mirror, I'd sprouted about twelve of them suckers overnight. Most men around here said just to roll them up and tuck 'em back in there, but I called horseshit. I wasn't an old man yet. I grabbed those suckers with my fingers and yanked, letting out a roar to emphasize my manliness—and maybe just a little bit of pain.

I sat up in my armchair, rubbing my lower back before wrestling myself up to my feet. The TV blared some infomercial about a blender. I dragged my feet across the carpet, shuffling them enough to give myself static shock when I reached the fridge.

"Bare," I muttered after opening the door.

What I wouldn't give for a nice home-cooked meal these days. The cafeteria here fed us old-people mush, assuming all of us had missing teeth. My teeth were luckily still all in my head, and I liked things that hadn't been smashed to death and easily digested. I grabbed the flannel blanket from the back of the couch and made my way to bed. I'd left my phone on my nightstand to charge, and already, I could see it was flashing at me from across the room. My grandchildren never learned how rude it was to text someone in the middle of the night.

I groaned as I fell back on the edge of the bed and checked the alarm clock. It was five fifteen in the morning, almost time for me to get up anyway. I sighed, hurling my feet on the bed and leaning back against the headboard. I picked up my phone, swiping left and right to try to find my text messages, but nothing came up. The only notification bubble I had appeared on Tinder. I pressed my finger to the app and saw that I had a new match.

# MAYDAY

I had swiped through a few profiles two days ago, but after hearing nothing back from any of them, I'd decided to take a break from it for a day or two—but only a day or two because who knew when I would lose all this testosterone that still coursed through my veins?

I pressed my matches and noticed immediately that it was who I'd half-feared and half-desired it to be—Marilyn Mae. I had known Marilyn from high school way, way, way back in the day. She had been an outspoken woman even back then. We were friendly throughout our years at that school, and during the time, rumors began about desegregating the schools. We had an open discussion in class about it, and afterward, I told her that I admired her for her bravery and honesty. It wasn't that I was a coward, but being a black boy back then had been risky, even among my peers. Marilyn, on the other hand, had been black girl magic. And from her picture on Tinder, she still was.

I had pushed her up against a locker and kissed her one day before I graduated and left. It was after study hall, and she had been rambling on and on about some situation I couldn't even remember. I only remembered I'd felt the need to shut her up with my lips, and I did. I had known it was my last chance. We never spoke after that. I wasn't sure if she had liked it or not, and I was too chicken to find out. I was a year ahead of her, so I had left school the following week, and that was the last time I'd seen her.

I smiled while reminiscing and scrolling through her profile, thinking of how to break the ice when a text bubble popped up on my message tabs.

> Marilyn: Clyde Jenkins! You old, sly devil. I guess you're not quiet Clyde anymore. I'd never have thought you the type to put yourself out there. Must be getting lonely at the end, or perhaps you just want someone to love and leave like you did me all those years ago.

*Me: Marilyn. I was hoping it was you who'd swiped me. I've changed a lot since high school, but I can see you haven't. Still got that sass I like. I'm sorry I was too much of a chickenshit back then. I've grown up to be a good man though.*

*Marilyn: Mmhmm. That's what they all say after they kiss and run. Tell me then, Mr. Perfect, how is life?*

*Me: I'm hardly perfect, but life is as good as it can get these days. How's your life? How many grandkids ya got now?*

*Marilyn: Too many. You?*

*Me: Same.*

*Marilyn: Do they come see you, or have they forgotten you exist?*

*Me: They do all right, I guess. I don't feel like I see them enough, but they're busy.*

*Marilyn: I know how you feel. So, you are getting lonely. That's what brought you on this app? I still am trying to figure it out. I think I swiped the wrong way on this picture of a catfish. He's been dinging my phone all damn night.*

*Me: Yeah, it took a while for me to get used to it. So far, I've only met a handful of women on here.*

*Marilyn: A handful? That is good at our age! Where can I find these people who are ready to hook up?*

*Me: Really? I'm right here.*

# MAYDAY

I patted my peter, which was twitching in my pants. *I still got it.* I smirked.

> *Marilyn: And that's all? I just tell you I want a man, and you jump right to it? What if I'm crazy?*

> *Me: Are you still the same Marilyn from back in the day who I had a crush on in high school? You know I liked you throughout the few years we went there?*

> *Marilyn: Yep. Same one. But, no, I didn't know you had a serious crush on me. I thought the kiss was just a passing one. Doesn't surprise me that you didn't speak up though. You were always shy.*

> *Me: Well, if you're the same, then I already know you're crazy.*

> *Marilyn: Careful.*

> *Me: See? And I'm not shy anymore. Bet you can see that too. I don't have much time left in life. It's too short for me to stick my head in the sand and wish for what I want. I go after it these days.*

> *Marilyn: And what is it you want?*

> *Me: You to come to game night. Think that's safe enough?*

> *Marilyn: Game night? Like a football game?*

> *Me: Bingo and cards. At Knotty Pines Retirement Center.*

> *Marilyn: Oh.*

I could detect disappointment in her message. Either that or *I* was disappointed that I'd had to tell her where I lived. Anytime I mentioned a retirement community, everyone would all of a sudden become sorrowful and pity me—and I did not like that. I was old but not too old to forget my dignity. I could still do things for myself. The retirement center was just a tool to help me along. It wasn't that bad. I had food and help when I needed it. But it was my grave before my grave, and it never felt like home.

> *Marilyn: I can play cards, but I'm not old enough for bingo, Clyde. I'll bring a game. I've heard about Knotty Pines. I'll liven it up. How's that sound? Old friends meeting for some games. Is that how this thing works? Did I just commit to a date?*
>
> *Me: Yep. You did. This Friday night after seven. Hey, do you still make those amazing cookies you used to bring to school?*
>
> *Marilyn: I do. But you'll have to butter me up before I go baking for a man again. I'll see you Friday at seven.*

I set my phone beside me and stretched. She'd told me I needed to butter her up, and *that* I could start on now at least. If I was going to see Marilyn May—and perhaps get into her girdle—I would need to get my body moving and ready. A woman like her would probably ride me hard and hang me out to dry.

I rubbed my sleepy eyes and stuck my hand down my pants before picking my phone back up and Googling dick exercises. I wanted to be prepared for anything.

# Three

## MARILYN

*K*lara came over to help me dress for my first date in forever. I didn't remember the last time I'd had to get all dolled up for a man, but I quickly remembered why I didn't do this sort of thing. Getting my hair done and making sure my nails weren't cracking was just another task I didn't have the energy to do.

"Remember, don't be as sassy as you are with me! You'll scare him off. What made you pick him anyway? How many other ones are you talking to?"

Klara was ironing a dress that I had worn to a funeral last year. Now, I would be hiking it up and showing my leg for Clyde in hopes that he would fix Roger and maybe, just maybe, show me some fun. But that was it. Friends with benefits I could do, but having a man to take care of was out of the question. I was done taking care of people. I could barely take care of myself these days. The arthritis in my hands made it hard to button, eat, and even raise my middle finger to flip off Gloria next door.

"Just the fact that we were in high school together and he kissed me once. We didn't know each other well, but he did admire me for this sassy mouth you're giving me crap about."

"Is that so? How do you know that?"

"Because he told me so one day after I mouthed off about racial injustices. I should have been a damn civil rights lawyer. I was a firecracker back then!" I stood in my granny panties and ancient bra, searching my drawer for any old jewelry I could find.

"Marilyn May, you are still a firecracker! You've probably even gotten sassier over the years. If he's into that, he's going to fall for you in no time. But is that what you want? What about the other men?" She set the hot iron down on the ironing board and shook out my dress.

"Well, let's see. I think I done swiped the entire Southern region. I'm talking to three men, Clyde included. The other two haven't sparked my interest as much. What's wrong with men? Do you have any idea how many pictures I swiped through with men standing in front of a toilet or holding up a fish? Not to mention, they take pictures of their dogs. I don't want to see their damn mutt's face. I want to see theirs. You know if they have a picture of their dog's mug, it means their mug must be too ugly to show. What do they think, that us women are stupid?"

I found an old costume piece of jewelry in the back of the drawer. I'd had it for longer than I could remember and never worn it. When I'd become newly single, I'd thought I would party all day and all night, but those times had been few and far between. I spent most of my time being a mother and grandmother to rambunctious children. Amazing children but wilder than rabid animals. I couldn't blame them though. If my mom had let me run crazy, then I would have had to. Not that I'd let them, but I had spoiled my babies.

"When they don't show their face, they are either ugly or married. Also, be careful. There're a lot of creeps out there. I'm glad you know this man. Otherwise, I'd be stalking you tonight to make sure you were safe."

"Child, please. I know how to take care of myself. Check it out." I pulled the cup down on my bra, revealing my knife.

"Oh my! What are you going to do if he cops a feel and slices his thumb open?" She handed me the dress.

"Tell him I got a Band-Aid at home and have him come here and fix my Roger first. Then, I might consider some hanky-spanky." I stepped into the pale blue dress and realized I'd put on ten pounds since I'd worn it last.

"I think it's called hanky-panky," she said, buttoning the jeweled buttons on the front of my dress.

I used to leave two unbuttoned, but these days, no one wanted to see these sad sacks hanging underneath.

"Not with me, it's not." I sucked in my breath, grabbing my sides. "I don't know if this is going to work. Hand me those hose over there in the bottom drawer. They're control-top and will suck all this in." I pointed toward my dresser before pinching my fat and wiggling it at her.

"Why didn't you try this one beforehand? How are you going to eat?" Klara fished through the drawer for a black pair of pantyhose and handed them to me.

"Who says I'm eating? It's a bingo date!" I rolled my eyes. "Stereotypical old-person stuff. But I got a trick up my sleeve—or in my purse."

"Let me guess. You're bringing your flask?"

"Yes. But that's not my trick. That's just me. My trick is, I'm bringing a card game that I swiped from my grandson last time he stayed here. Ever heard of Cards Against Humanity?"

"Oh, gosh! Yes! Are you seriously bringing Cards Against Humanity to the old folks' home? You're going to get kicked out! That game has some nasty stuff in it!"

I sat myself on the edge of the bed as Klara helped roll the pantyhose over the bulging veins in my legs, courtesy of all those children I claimed to love.

"It will probably liven up the place. I never played it. I just read the directions and cards. They made me laugh, and when you get as old as we are, you need all the laughter you can get. It's depressing, not being able to do some things. I'll be laughing with my sassy mouth to the grave!" I groaned as she pulled me to my feet and helped pull up the tight hose that sucked in my sweet-tea-and-whiskey gut. Once again, I blamed that pooch on my children too. Because of them, I drank.

"I wouldn't expect any less from you. Now, go have a good time tonight—but not too good of a time. I ordered you a driver, so one less thing you have to worry about. He will be here soon and will stay there all night until you are ready to leave." She smoothed the back of my dress and held me at arm's length.

"What, you don't think I can drive?" I crossed my arms over my chest and narrowed my eyes.

Driving was at least one thing I could still do, and I was grateful for that. Losing my license would be a kick in the ego. Some days, I liked to hop in my car and joyride out to the country even if I hugged the steering wheel for dear life and people lined up, honking behind me. I used to have a lead foot, but now, everything moved slow. Yet another thing people forgot to mention about aging. Everything was slow—and I meant it. Slow to wake up, slow to eat, slow to drive, slow to fall asleep, and slow to move my bowels.

"No, I didn't say that. But I just don't want to worry about you. Now, take a sweater, dear, and don't stay up all night." She laughed and put her arms around me. "Good luck on your first Tinder date, Ms. Marilyn May! Don't drink too much out of that flask. I need details for my research!"

"I can't promise I'll behave, but I'll be safe. Don't worry about me, honey. Go back to Chris and get started on those babies." I hugged her back, grateful for her keeping me company ever since my family had left town.

"On it."

# MAYDAY

I gathered my things as we walked to the front door, and I waved her good-bye. My driver was already parked on the street, waiting.

"Good-bye, Roger, you piece of shit!" I called behind me as I locked the door and stepped out and into the night.

Roger clanked in response, puttering out in a deflated hiss.

*Men ...*

I hadn't thought I was nervous about meeting Clyde until we pulled up to the doors of the retirement center, and he was standing right there at the entrance, waiting on me. He stood tall, straight-backed, no cane. I felt a flutter down below from something I'd thought died long ago.

"I'll wait right up there for you, Ms. May. If I doze off, just tap the window and hop right in," the driver said as Clyde rushed to my door and opened it for me.

I nodded at my driver and took a deep breath.

"Marilyn. It's been far too long. You look just as beautiful as the last day I saw you in school," Clyde said, giving me his hand and pulling me up. His hands were strong, wrapped around my frail, arthritic fingers. It only took one swift tug, and he had me up and falling into his arms.

"Glory be! You move fast!" I said, awkwardly hugging him like I had intended to do instead of tripping into an embrace.

"I take vitamins. Keeps my heart going strong." He smiled, peeling himself away from me and stepping back.

His slacks hugged his trim waist, and the top two buttons on his collar were left undone, showing me a peek of silver fur—like a wolf.

"That dress fits you like a glove." He whistled, sticking his hands in his pockets and rocking back on his heels. His eyes grazed over my face, my shoulders, my dress, and right down to my orthopedic shoes.

"Thanks. You look the same as ever too. Now, are we going to stand here in this cold, or should I have brought my parka too?" I hooked my arm around his and nodded toward the doors. I hadn't wanted to touch him or give him any ideas, but my knees had begun to shake with tremors that sometimes curled around my joints. I gritted my teeth and hobbled next to him, hoping he wouldn't notice.

"Now, I know proper first dates are normally out at a nice restaurant, but this place isn't so bad. Game night can get pretty lively. It's usually the liveliest night we have. I thought you'd like to see it. Do you know how to play poker?" He patted my hand that was curled around his toned bicep and led me toward an open room packed full of people at tables.

"Of course I know how to play that game. But … I did bring something with me, just in case you're interested. I didn't know how dead this place would be. I wanted to bring some fun. But you said it's lively, so …" My eyes took in all the old farts around me.

I was indeed in the middle of a geriatric party. Some people were laughing so hard that they coughed until they turned purple. Others wheeled around in their wheelchairs, throwing their hands in the air. One man stood up, pointing a finger at another man and cursing before a nurse stepped in and sent them to different tables.

"What did you bring? Pot? Seems like all these geezers are doing that these days since it's being legalized everywhere. Ever seen a ninety-nine-year-old stoner?" Clyde nodded toward a table in the corner.

"It's not pot, and no, I didn't know a ninety-nine-year-old had the lung capacity to smoke that shit."

"That one right there does. His name is Calvin. That's our table. The lady next to him is Wanda, and then you have Cletus beside her. That's her husband. And lastly, you have my good friend Paco. He doesn't speak much English, but he's cool. They're all cool. I'm sure they'll be down with whatever you brought." Clyde led me to the back table and introduced me to his friends.

"What did he say your name was?" Wanda called loudly.

"I'm Marilyn," I shouted, knowing a hard-of-hearing old coot when I saw one.

"Marilyn." Wanda smiled, crinkling her face up like an old, worn-out sock puppet.

"Marilyn here said she brought us something to liven up our night." Clyde pulled a chair out for me and helped me down into it.

My knees still shook, knocking bruises into each other. He rested his palm on my shoulder and gave it a calming pat. Somehow, he must have known I was nervous and having issues. I didn't know how, as I had a poker face like no one. I could smile through a root canal. No one moved my face. It was part of the reason black don't crack. At least, for me.

"Reefer?" Calvin's eyes lit up like I'd just given him another twenty years on this earth. He looked like he had all of twenty minutes left.

"No, not reefer." I pursed my lips into a thin line. "A game. Cards Against Humanity. Clyde invited me to game night, and I thought we could mix it up. It's an adult game. Ever heard of it?" I reached into my purse and pulled out the card deck.

"An adult game?" Wanda yelled right next to me.

"Shh! Damn it, Wanda! It's you that's hard of hearing, woman! Not her. You don't have to shout! I could probably hear you from clear cross this cafeteria!" Cletus shook his head.

"Well, you just met her. How do you know she ain't hard of hearing?" Wanda turned toward me. "Am I speaking too loud for you?"

Her voice rattled my head, making my eyes cross. I clenched my teeth, feeling her screech into my nerves—my last nerve.

"Honey, I think you could wake the dead. Like that one over there," I said, nodding toward a woman slumped over in her chair, her jaw hanging open, snoring.

"What did she say?" Wanda turned toward Cletus, who shook his head.

"She said, you're a tad loud, dear."

Paco's head bobbed up and down. I wasn't sure if he was agreeing with us or had the old-person shakes.

"Right. Marilyn, tell us how to play this game." Clyde winked at me.

I hadn't had a man wink at me in ages. My breath caught in my throat with the way he looked at me with those sparkling eyes. He didn't look a day over twenty-five. Well, his eyes didn't. The rest of his face was barely lined with smile lines and crow's-feet. Again, he proved my theory that black don't crack.

I dealt the cards, telling everyone how to play and warning them that some cards could be offensive.

"I'm not easily offended, dude," Calvin said, flipping over his cards and scratching his messy head.

"Oh my!" Wanda laughed, nudging Cletus and showing him a card.

"You're not supposed to show me!" Cletus rubbed his palm across his brow and sighed.

"How could I not? We did this the other day." Wanda sat up straight in her chair and smirked.

Clyde shot me a look over his cards and winked again. I squirmed in my seat. It wasn't Wanda's loud voice waking me up; it was Clyde's gaze, touch, and the way his voice glided over words instead of sounding like the normal old-man's voice. They often sounded like they had a choking bullfrog stuck in their throat. But Clyde, his voice was music to my ears.

I reached for my flask in my purse, took a swig, offered it around the table, and went to work.

"I'll start," I muttered, letting the warm whiskey wash over me, settling my nerves. "Everyone, don't show your cards. Put your best card in the middle, facedown. Okay, here goes." I pulled a card from the stacked deck and read aloud, "*What's that smell?*"

"Cletus," Wanda shouted.

"No! No! That's the question. Now, fill it with your card." I shook my hand, fanning the flames from my face. Things were about to get awkward fast. I waited for everyone to put a card down before I picked them up and began.

"What's that smell?" I said again, reading the first card. "*Half-assed foreplay.*"

"Mine! Mine! I told you that's what we did!" Wanda shouted.

"You aren't supposed to say which is yours! Jeez, woman!" Cletus buried his head in his hands.

"Moving on. What's that smell? *Crystal meth.*" I nodded my head, picking up another card and stifling my laughter. "What's that smell? *A smiling black man, a Latina businesswoman, a cool Asian, and some whites.*" I looked around the corner of the table, noticing Cletus's smug face.

"That was terrible," Clyde said. "But I like it. Keep going."

"What's that smell?" I asked again, taking the remaining two cards. "*Making the penises kiss,*" I read aloud before what I'd just read registered in my mind. I clutched my chest. "Oh my gosh!"

The men at the table shifted in their seats, wincing—all but Paco, who looked satisfied but clueless with what had just happened. It must be his card.

"What's that smell?" I continued, "*Hope.*" I caught Clyde's eye. My heart fluttered under his gaze. It had to be his card. "That one was deep," I sighed. "I have some tough choices. Last one," I said, picking up the last card and turning it over in my hand. "What's that smell? *Balls.*" I cringed.

The table was silent until Calvin burst into laughter, making us all feel safe enough to do the same.

Wanda slapped her palm on the table. "This is nasty! What else ya got? Clyde, this one's a keeper. She's just like one of us. You were right!"

The corner of my mouth twitched as I tried to conceal my smile with a poker face. I wondered what Clyde had been telling them. "Balls wins."

"Woohoo!" said Calvin. "That one was mine! So, I get to do the next question?"

I nodded at him, taking my flask out again and passing it around.

"*This month's* Cosmo," Calvin read, "*Spice up your sex life by bringing* blank *into the bedroom.*"

Clyde grinned and immediately threw a card down.

I checked my cards and didn't have anything too exciting, so I put down, *A mopey zoo lion.*

"That it? Let's go." Calvin began to read the cards. "This month's *Cosmo*: Spice up your sex life by bringing *a sad hand job* into the bedroom. Jeez, that sounds depressing." He continued, "Spice up your sex life by bringing *a grandma* into the bedroom."

"Whoop, whoop!" Wanda danced in her chair, snapping her fingers in the air. "Can't out-kink a granny who has been through the free-love era," she shouted.

The tables nearby grew silent as they turned their attention to us.

"Spice up your sex life by bringing *an erection that lasts longer than four hours*!" Calvin laughed.

"Back in my day—" Cletus started.

"Just hush. No one wants to hear about your old, droopy dangalang." Wanda held her hand out, motioning for the flask. I passed it to her, feeling a bit looser myself.

"Spice up your sex life by bringing *an endless stream of diarrhea* into the bedroom," Calvin choked out. He gripped the card, falling back in his chair and laughing. "That's what happens when you eat this shit food they serve here!"

"Wow. I had no idea you were this dirty, Marilyn." Clyde rubbed his chin, erasing a grin off of his face.

"I'm not usually! It's the game, I swear! I didn't know it was this dirty either! I stole it from my grandson! Kids these days!" I rolled my eyes and fell back onto the excuse I knew old people loved.

"Kids these days," everyone agreed.

"Last one. Spice up your sex life by bringing a … *big black dick* into the bedroom." Calvin blew out a breath while I held mine. That was the bottom card he had read. The one that Clyde had so quickly thrown down with a grin.

I glanced from under my eyelashes, and sure enough, he still wore a smirk. The shriveled raisin in my control-top pantyhose swelled to a prune. Which reminded me that I needed to buy prune juice because I was plumb out.

*What the hell?*

"This is just wrong. Wrong. Wrong." Wanda laughed. "Can't be my husband's card," she slurred, eyeing Clyde up and down.

"I'm going to go with an endless stream of diarrhea. Who did that one?" Calvin pressed the card on the table.

Paco raised his hand, bobbing in his seat.

"I don't think he can speak English well. How's this going to work?" Cletus looked from me to Paco.

"What are you all doing over here?" A nurse stepped up to our table and took the flask from Wanda's hand. "You know alcohol isn't allowed on the premises!"

"I'm sorry, Ms. Jenn. It's mine. I snuck it in. I only wanted to pretend like it was old times since we never know which one of us will be found dead in bed tomorrow." Clyde's bottom lip poked out into a quiver.

"Nonsense. You all look healthy enough to me. Especially if you're able to laugh as loud as you were over this." Her chin jutted toward the pile of cards.

"Care to play?" Wanda hiccuped.

"No. And I think it's about time to break it up. You should get some water and some sleep. Your body is going to feel this tomorrow. Besides, it's almost time to shut it down." Ms. Jenn began taking our cards and stuffing them back into the box.

"We just got started!" Calvin cried.

"Well, when you break the rules and start drinking, there're consequences!" She looked me over twice. "Are you new?"

"I'm visiting. They're my cards." My voice fell flat as I snatched the deck from her hands.

"Visiting hours are almost up. Better get yourself ready to go!" Ms. Jenn looked to Clyde and narrowed her eyes before turning on her heels to leave.

"Come on. I'll walk you out of this jail. You don't want to stay here any longer than you have to." Clyde pushed himself up and off of his chair, groaning.

"It was nice to meet you all." I gathered my purse and waved good-bye.

They thanked me for the game and the booze before letting me go. Wanda was already slumped over on Cletus, dozing off.

"I didn't mean to get anyone in trouble!" I whispered to Clyde, who led me to the door, holding me around the waist.

"You didn't. We haven't had a night like that in forever. I don't think I've ever heard Wanda or Calvin laugh that hard. You even got a smile out of Cletus and Paco. That's saying something!"

The front doors automatically opened, letting the chilled air inside the breezeway. I shivered, ready to take another swig of my flask as soon as I got into my ride.

"I feel like I just got here! I didn't know they had rules like that. Who does she think she is, breaking up our fun?" I looked up at Clyde, but before I could register what he was about to do, his lips pressed hard against mine.

My eyes flew open as I stared into his freshly smoothed cheek. He smelled of aftershave—and not the typical old-man stuff, but like a new man, a sexy and young one—and I'd love to have that scent in my sheets.

*Just what the hell is this? Have him in my sheets?*

I pulled away, swaying. "I think I took a bit too many sips of the flask."

He put his arms around me and brought me into his chest. My hands reached around his tight waist and up his back. I couldn't stop them. They had a mind of their own. I stroked his firm back, gently running my palm over his shoulder blades and down, down, down until I could squeeze his apple bottom.

"Marilyn!" he squealed.

"Yes?" I smirked. I'd definitely had enough whiskey.

He leaned down, whispering in my ear, "Do it again."

I rubbed his bottom, thankful it wasn't drooping like most men's asses my age. I had seen one that looked like a water balloon melting down the back of his legs. Another looked like a sack of marbles. But Clyde's butt felt like a ripe peach.

"I've got to go." I backed away. "Sorry the night got cut short." My breath became ragged, but not like I was damn near a heart attack. I knew those signs from my recent scare earlier in the year.

*If this man puts me in the hospital with his wolfish stare, it might be worth it. Damn it! Worth it? No. This is why I don't date men! They always put me through some shit! NOT worth it! NOT! NOT! NOT!* I told my dumbass self.

"When can I see you again? We didn't even get to know each other!" Clyde called out as I hobbled my wobbly knees to my ride.

I mentally cursed myself for even attempting a date night. My mind and body couldn't handle these emotions.

"Text me." My voice fell flat as I pulled the car door open and lowered myself in, waving good-bye before shutting it.

"Ready for home!" I told the driver, who was groggily waking from a nap.

"All right. How did it go?" he responded, pulling away.

I looked in his rearview mirror. Clyde still stood where I'd left him, watching us go.

"It was a visit to an old folks' home. How do you think it went?" I muttered, folding my arms and settling back for a quick nap.

# Four

## CLYDE

*I* had tossed and turned all night after Marilyn left. The whiskey had given me heartburn, and the way Marilyn's hips had swayed when she walked to her ride awakened every part of me—especially my nether regions.

For an old man, I still had it. I didn't need Viagra. Though I had heard from a friend that it would make me feel like an eighteen-year-old again. My ego wouldn't let me try it, but for Marilyn, I might be able to swallow my pride with that little blue pill. I wanted to impress her. That smart mouth of hers had me heated more than that whiskey flask she'd snuck into the retirement home.

I rolled myself out of bed, grumbling and longing for the smell of bacon and eggs in the morning. Instead, I smelled nothing but old man—me. I cursed myself for letting that happen. When I had been younger, I remembered my grandpa having a distinct old-man smell. It was as if he'd bathed in a dustpan and sponged himself with stale bread. He'd just smelled old. There was no describing that scent other than the smell of an old man. Last night, I had doused myself in so much aftershave that I thought if someone lit a match around me, then I'd surely catch fire. At least, I hoped I'd covered the old man scent up, and Marilyn hadn't noticed I was stale.

I pushed my heels into the floor and did a few morning stretches, followed by fifteen jumping jacks, a plank, and running in place for a minute. I had to get the blood flowing. Otherwise, I would croak before feeling a woman in my bed again. And for ol' Clydesdale, that wasn't happening. I had gone through too many years of deprivation to go out without a bang. Literally.

I pulled the blinds open on my one and only window and looked out over the parking lot. The sun rose above the horizon, painting the sky a pinkish hue. I lived for sunrises. Back at my old home, the majority of my rooms had faced toward the sun. Every morning, I would wake up to catch those cotton candy–colored rays scattered through the clouds. But sunrises were much sweeter, sharing them with a sweetheart in my arms.

I sighed and sat back down on the edge of my bed. I pulled out my wife's picture from my nightstand to catch her up on my life's events. I would do that now and then. I wished I could visit her grave, but that was out of the question. I could no longer drive. It hadn't happened overnight. I'd lost my ability to drive gradually over the last year. It wasn't like I had dementia or anything like that, but my skills had taken a nosedive a few years ago. After running Stop signs, hitting curbs, and becoming lost once, my children had forced me to give up one of the last pieces of independence I had. And I was still upset about it.

"Katherine, I met a woman. You wouldn't like her," I told the photo of her I held in my hands. It had been taken back in the '70s when she was young and still not wild.

"She's mouthy, rude, feisty, and everything you never let yourself be. I take that back. Remember that one time I forgot your parents' anniversary? That weekend, you were a lot like her. You might not remember, but I was all over you that weekend even though you wanted nothing to do with me." I laughed, smiling down into those big brown eyes.

"Anyway, I just wanted to let you know that I'm doing okay. I know when you left, you worried over me having someone to take care of me, and I can take care of myself—kind of. I do miss your cooking. I've not had a home-cooked meal since Thanksgiving when our crazy kids came up here. They call once in a while, but they have their own lives, and I'll not push them to come to this depressing dead zone.

"It gets lonely sometimes, but I'm trying to reach out and fill my days and nights. If anything, for a homemade casserole at least. I know you're laughing wherever you are. You always knew the way to my heart was through my stomach … and maybe through my penis, too, but you didn't ever try that. I know you're laughing again. I'm glad we had that kind of relationship where we could at least be honest.

"So, do you think you can send me some help down here? I know you're up there with your ex-boyfriend. That one with the muscles you joked about. I saw his obituary years ago and never mentioned it. I didn't want to make you sad. But I know you're probably getting frisky with musclehead. Send me some luck, fairy dust, or just a big sign for me to have some fun too. I'm afraid I don't have much longer. People are dropping left and right around here, and I worry that I'll be the next. I know; I know. I'll keep my cholesterol in check. Love you."

I tucked the photograph back inside my nightstand and shuffled my feet toward the kitchen for a cold bowl of bran cereal.

I woke from my afternoon nap to the sound of my phone buzzing beside me. I held it up close to my face and squinted my eyes, reading Marilyn's name. My brows shot up into my hairline as I lost my grip on the phone and watched it slide between my recliner cushion.

"Damn it," I moaned, sticking my palm between the arm and cushion and quickly fishing it out between Cheetos crumbs and a disintegrating tissue. "Hello? Hello? You there?" I answered.

"Course I'm here. I called you. Are you there? As in all in the head? Did you smoke some of that wacky tobaccy from Calvin?" Marilyn said.

"No, I didn't. I was just half-asleep when you called. I must have been dreaming." I cleared my throat.

"Taking a nap? Let me guess. You are in front of a TV, in an old, worn-down recliner. You got an empty freezer meal tray beside you, and your remote is in your lap. You were watching some news channel. I'm not going to say which one because if we have a difference in politics, I'm hanging up now. I don't have time for that crazy mess, so I don't even want to know."

"Then, I'll keep my mouth shut. And it's not an empty freezer-tray meal. They feed us here. It's an empty tray from the cafeteria. Well, it's not fully empty. I get tired of eating all this damn mush they serve."

"What kind of mush do they serve? You don't have family bringing you food? Or you can't get up and cook your own?"

I sighed into the phone. "I don't cook much. I never learned how really. I can heat things, and I can grill, except I don't do that anymore either, given my living circumstances. Besides, it's a little depressing, cooking for one. My family doesn't see me often enough for me to make meals for them, too, and they rarely bring anything, save for Thanksgiving or Christmas dinner. So, I eat mush. Corn mush, bean mush, bread mush, and casserole mush."

"Good Lawd! That sounds terrible. You mean to tell me, you haven't had a home-cooked meal in a while? Is that right?"

I shot my eyes over to the nightstand drawer and grinned, mouthing a silent, *Thank you*, to Katherine's picture inside.

"Nope. No home-cooking. I think it's why I'm all dried up and wasting away." I pouted.

"Hmm. How about I cook you a meal to make up for what trouble I got us into last night? I called to make sure everything was all right and apologize again for the booze. I'd had no idea it was against the rules. But since you mentioned not eating a proper meal, I think I can fix that."

"Marilyn Mae, are you trying to get into my pants?" I laughed.

"Clyde, if I want to get into those old grandpa drawers of yours, I'd cup your drooping jewels in my hand and let you know. Besides, I was wondering if you could look at something for me. Maybe this can be a trade-off too. I know you had your own business, doing contract work for new homes."

"How did you—" I started.

"Google. Don't you think I screen every weirdo on the internet before I even think about meeting them? Doesn't matter if we knew each other back in high school. You could still be a serial killer and need me for my kidney. My friend Klara taught me how to Google people. Looks like you did all right. And not only that, but I could use a friend like you who knows a thing or two about home stuff. Know anything about radiators?"

"Yes. What kind?" I put the footrest down on my recliner and pushed myself up, needing to pace the floor.

Anytime I had to think, I had to walk. Katherine used to tease me about it, saying I had worn a track down in our carpet during those years I worked to get the business off the ground.

"How should I know what kind? It's old and a piece of shit. That's what kind it is."

"All right, I'll take a look at it," I said before realizing that I was committing to going to her place and I couldn't even drive. Panic rose in my chest, making me breathe hard. I didn't want to tell her I was too much of an old man to drive. I didn't like to let anyone know that. When I'd lost my license, I'd lost a piece of myself. I felt officially old.

"Great. I can make a Sunday supper this weekend if you'd like."

I gritted my teeth, wrestling with an internal struggle against my pride and her cooking. "Sunday, ya say? I'll be there. What time do we eat? Five o'clock?" I walked from the kitchen to the living room and back, which was all of nine steps.

"Yep. You don't have any health concerns I should be aware of, do you? Like, are your teeth falling out of your head? Do I need to serve you mush too? You know I got this special glue bond for mine, so I can tear into a steak or whatever I want. I can let you borrow some."

"No. Please don't make mush. Still got my teeth. I do have high cholesterol, but you don't have to worry about me. One meal ain't gonna kill me."

"As long as it doesn't kill you before you take a look at this no-good heater of mine, I'll see what I can do. I'm supposed to watch my cholesterol too. We all do at this wonderful age. Sunday at five, Clyde. See you then."

Marilyn hung up the phone before I could respond. I texted her immediately, telling her she'd forgotten to tell me her address. She replied that I could look her up in the phone book like a normal person. I had a stack of them under my bathroom sink. When duty called, I'd flip through them while sitting on the throne.

I grabbed one of the massive yellow books from under the sink and walked back to my recliner, plopping down in a grunt. I flipped to car services before I checked for Marilyn's address, and I reminded myself that she hadn't driven here. There was no sense in my shame if that old bat couldn't get around either. I dialed the number for a ride and set up an appointment for next Sunday before booking a haircut and shave and hobbling down the hall to tell all my friends about my date.

I stood in front of my bathroom mirror, double-checking that my nose hairs and ear hairs weren't sticking out all over the place. I ran a dab of pomade through my hair, spritzed myself with cologne so old that it had yellowed in the bottle, and sprinkled foot powder in my musty shoes. I dressed in my Sunday best, knowing how mature Southern women felt about Sunday supper. Before I walked out of my room, I grabbed my fedora from the coatrack and gently sat it atop my head.

Sunday supper was a big deal for the families around here. Back when she had been alive, Katherine had usually invited over neighbors and people from church during those times. I hadn't been fond of having so many people at the house, eating up all my cornbread and crumb cake, but it'd made her happy to host, so I'd kept my trap shut. My mouth watered as I imagined a warm meal with Marilyn for dessert.

I checked the time on my watch, slipped my coat on, and headed out the door. Calvin stood in the hallway, high-fiving me as I walked by him.

"Get it, Clyde!" he said, spanking the air and thrusting his hips.

"Smoking that shit again?" I raised my eyebrows, continuing past him.

"Yep," Calvin called after me.

"Just don't break a hip, moving like that! Or burn a lung," I yelled down the hall, exiting the doors.

One of the residents, Martha, had her wheelchair parked in front of the entrance. She kept backing up and pulling forward, making the automatic doors open and shut, all while laughing hysterically. I dodged the crazy lady and exited the building. My driver was waiting out front. I'd ordered a town car so that I could show up in style. Having owned my own business had left me with plenty of money to spend when I needed to even if I was a penny-pinching son of a bitch.

I gently lowered myself into the seat and gave my driver Marilyn's address before giving him The Grump. The Grump was something all old people inherited, I'd learned. We had this stink face that a lot of us wore permanently. The Grump was a mixture of a snarl, a nose crinkle, furrowed brows, and a sour mouth. Usually, Grumps would say things like "back in my day" or complain about anything and everything. Putting on The Grump was a surefire way for me not to be bothered, and the last thing I wanted on my way to my hot date was small talk. I was too busy in my head, planning on how I could bang Marilyn on a full stomach.

I rubbed my belly as it let out a loud, rude noise. I hadn't eaten since breakfast. I wanted to save all my room for my next meal—and again, so I didn't feel too fat to tango. Usually, after a large meal, I'd fall asleep. I couldn't be doing that at a woman's house even if she had a cozy blanket and a worn-in couch. I wouldn't let myself get too comfortable. I reminded myself that I was on the prowl to go out with a bang, and being in Marilyn's arms was the goal—after dinner.

The driver pulled onto Marilyn's street and slowly crept past house after house that looked older than me.

"This is it, Mr. Clyde. Would you like me to wait here or pick you up at a certain time?" he asked.

"Here." I handed him a fifty-dollar bill. "Go get you some dinner and then come back and wait for me, please."

I tipped my hat, slung my coat over my shoulder, and sauntered up the stairs and onto the porch of Marilyn May, high school and nursing-home badass. I knocked three times, shivering in the cold but stubbornly not putting on my jacket. I wanted to stand here, looking like I'd walked straight out of an old heartthrob movie with my coat slung over my shoulder while leisurely leaning up against the rotting column on her porch. I was old but still cool.

Marilyn opened the door and smiled. "Clyde, come in. I want you to meet my friends."

*Friends? So, this isn't a date? I'm not going to get laid?*

"Oh." My voice dropped, but I kept a smile plastered on my face. "Sure, sure." My heart fell into the bottom of my gut as disappointment overtook me. I took my hat off and hung it on a coatrack similar to the one I had back home.

Marilyn introduced me to her neighbor Gloria and a younger couple named Chris and Klara. All three sat on a couch, facing me. Chris stood to shake my hand, but I motioned for Klara and Gloria to sit.

"Don't get up for me!" I grinned, reaching over to shake their hands too.

"Food's ready now. Might as well get up," Marilyn said. Her black dress swayed as her hips sashayed into the kitchen.

I heard a quiet giggle come from behind me and turned to see Chris catch my eye and wink. Klara was behind, helping Gloria off the couch.

"I was in that same position not too long ago. Not with Marilyn, of course, but Klara. I recognize that look," he whispered. "Just keep trying and don't do anything stupid like I did."

"What did you do?" I whispered back.

"Almost lost her for good, being a dumbass. So, don't be a dumbass, and you're golden. Ms. May is a lot to handle. Godspeed, Clyde," Chris said, stepping in front of me and quickly offering to help Ms. May serve several dishes that were laid out across her countertop.

The scent of roasted meat and gravy filled the air as I absentmindedly let out a groan.

I cleared my throat. "Excuse me. It smells divine in here, Marilyn! What in the world is that you're making? A five-star culinary institute come in here and do all this for you? This smells and looks amazing. I bet it tastes even better!" I pulled out a chair toward the end of the table and what I hoped was nearby her seat, so I could at least play footsie.

"Someone cook for me? Ha! No one can do this, baby." She paused in her step, the word *baby* hanging in the air. "I mean, I've been cooking for a long time. Ain't no restaurant going to compare," she continued, bringing over a plate of vegetables and setting it in the center of the table.

Chris brought over a heavy roasting pan full of juicy meat and set it down before going back for a bowl of mashed potatoes.

"Instant?" I looked at Marilyn, teasing.

"You're treading hot water. Those are from scratch, and if I could have picked the potatoes with these arthritic hands, I would have done that too." Marilyn wagged her finger at me.

"You know she is stubborn enough to do that, even with her hands," Gloria said, finally catching up to the table and sitting beside me.

"She is," both Klara and Chris answered in unison, laughing.

"This ain't gonna be a *pick on Marilyn* dinner convo," Marilyn said, setting a casserole dish full of something creamy in front of me. "Or else it will be the last time y'all eat like this. I might crush up some of that oleander Klara put in my backyard."

"Oleander? That's poison!" I swallowed hard.

"Exactly." She smiled sweetly.

Klara explained to me how she knew Ms. May and all the work she did, volunteering with the floral shop, while Chris and Marilyn continued prepping the table and pouring glasses of sweet tea.

"I never even knew we had such a thing in Memphis, but it sounds wonderful. Our retirement community could use something like that. Fresh flowers might brighten that coffin-like place up." I shook my head.

"That's actually a brilliant idea, Clyde. I'm going to see what I can do about it. I never thought of that!" Klara unfolded a napkin and set it on her lap.

Marilyn settled into the chair at the end of the table, next to me, and held out her hand. "We say grace."

"Absolutely." I nodded, taking her hand.

This was my opportunity to let her know how I really felt even if it was during the Lord's prayer. Gloria stuck out her hand, reaching for my other one. I closed my eyes as Marilyn began to pray. I peeked out from under my lashes to make sure no one was looking before I softly caressed Marilyn's hand by circling my finger on her palm.

"Glory be!" Marilyn's voice rang out, making us all jump and look around before bowing our heads again. "Excuse me. That spirit got ahold of me! What I mean to say is, thank you, Lawd!" she continued.

I stroked her finger back and forth as her voice wobbled through the prayer—slowly, as if she didn't want it to stop. I firmly clutched her hand in mine, feeling her bony knuckles clutch back.

My old boy down below began to awaken just as I felt a hand on my thigh. But it was on my left side, not my right side, where Marilyn sat. I peeked over toward Gloria, who licked her lips at me and winked.

*Jeez! These women are more deprived than the old bags at Knotty Pines.*

"Amen!" Marilyn shouted as Gloria recoiled her hand back and sat up straight in her chair.

"Praise Jesus!" Gloria fanned herself.

"Beautiful as always, Ms. May." Klara reached across, patting Marilyn's arm.

"Now, let's dig in!" Chris pushed himself up off his seat and began cutting into the pot roast and putting it on everyone's plates as dish after dish was passed around.

I had no shame when it came to home-cooking. I piled my plate high and dug in. I had already prepared myself before leaving my place by taking antacids and Beano. I'd not be in pain or an old windbag while I had Marilyn alone. At least, I had thought I'd have her alone. I hadn't planned on having company. To get her alone now would require some shenanigans.

I gobbled up my food and answered questions about my life in between bites. Gloria seemed particularly interested in life at the retirement community. I caught Marilyn staring at her over the rim of her sweet tea glass as she slowly sipped her drink. The look in her eyes sent a shiver up my spine, as I felt trapped in the tension between the two. I gulped my tea down hard and rubbed my belly.

"Phew. That was the best meal I've had in years, Marilyn. Maybe forever. I don't ever think I've tried a casserole like that!" I said, nodding at the almost-empty casserole dish.

"You haven't. It's my secret recipe." Marilyn set her napkin on the table.

"Yeah, I think she used to call it her Come Back recipe. As in she feeds it to a man, and he is sure to come back." Gloria smirked. "Gotta have some kind of trick up that sleeve when you have a mouth like hers."

"Gloria, did you take your medication?" Marilyn sat her elbows on the table and leaned forward with a snarl.

My eyes widened as I looked at Chris for help.

"Gosh! Look at the time! It's so late. Time for us all to head home. Come on, Gloria. We will walk you home." Chris stood up in his chair and came around to the other side of the table, pulling Gloria to her feet.

"What about dessert? I didn't bust my ass in this kitchen for no one to eat it!" Marilyn huffed, looking around at everyone who seemed to be abandoning the table in record time.

"Clyde will eat it, I'm sure. He still has to teach you about your heater. I'll pack this up while Chris walks Gloria home." Klara quickly grabbed the dishes and began putting lids on them before stuffing them in the refrigerator.

"Let me at least help with the dishes," I said, carrying plates to the sink.

"Thank you," Klara said. "But I got it. Why don't you and Marilyn go into the living room, and she can show you that heater?"

I nodded, pulling at my collar. "It seems pretty hot in here to me but will do," I whispered.

Klara shot me a knowing look.

Marilyn sat at the table, sipping her sweet tea.

"Come on, dear. Show me this problem you have."

"Which one?" she answered.

"The heater. You said it's giving you some trouble." I took her hand in mine and pulled her up to her feet, gently placing my palm on her back.

"Oh, yes, Roger."

"Roger?" I stroked her lower back, trying to calm her nerves, which were clearly rattled with whatever was going on between Gloria and her.

"That's what I call my radiator. Named after a man because he acts like a man. Pissing me off and all. Should have named him Gloria—"

"Okay! She's out of here." Chris barged back through the front door. "And so are we! In just a minute. Let me get this all cleaned up for you." He held up his index finger and disappeared into the kitchen to help Klara.

"What's going on with her and you? Y'all aren't friends? I'd think anyone at Sunday supper would be friendly with you." I followed Marilyn to the corner of the room, where Roger clanked obnoxiously.

"It's complicated. But it all boils down to jealousy of everything. We've always had a rivalry. There was a time I thought she might have been shacking up with that crusty old ex of mine, but who knows? I can't let that old fart bother me. I saw the way she looked at you though." She pursed her lips and crossed her arms across her chest, staring at me with a look that I thought would melt me into ashes—that was, if this old furnace didn't beforehand.

"We're gone!" Klara called. "See ya tomorrow!"

Chris and Klara hurried out the door, slamming it shut before we could answer back.

I turned my attention back to Marilyn and threw my hands in the air. "I saw that look she was giving me too. I'm not sure who is feistier. You or her!"

"Me," she growled, slipping her finger between my pants and shirt and pulling me toward her.

# Five

## MARILYN

*I* sat on the edge of my bed, looking over at the old man next to me. He snored loudly through his nose, making a whistling sound that sounded like a train tooting its horn. I had worn him out last night. I took a deep breath and grinned, thinking about all we had done. My body ached in places I'd forgotten I had, which at least meant I was still alive.

*"Marilyn, it's been a while for me," Clyde mumbled. "I'm not as young as I used to be."*

*"You think it's been a while for you? You have no idea. I've not ridden the pink rocket in so long. I'm afraid I might blow out dust once you stick it in there. Doesn't mean I ain't going to try to jump your bones anyway." I slid my hand down the front of his slacks, noticing that he'd unbuttoned the top button after dinner.*

*His man cannon was soft in my hand but slowly growing stiffer. Or as stiff as an old man's willy could get.*

*"Well, I'll say, woman. You are something else." He shook his head. "You really want to go down this road? At our age?" His hands reached up, gently cradling my face.*

*I mentally thanked Klara for plucking those damn stray, gnarly gray hairs that had kept popping up on the tip of my chin, right where he rested his palms.*

*I hesitated, knowing that getting in a relationship at this ripe old age was risky business. One of us could drop dead and leave the other heartbroken for the rest of our days. But we didn't have to get into a relationship. We could just be bed partners.*

*"To be honest with you, I just wanted my heater looked at and maybe some company. But after the game night at your place, I realized my body isn't ready to get cold and fall into a grave. I still want to feel alive. Can you make me feel alive, Clyde?" My hand clutched firmer around his old peter.*

*He squealed like a stuck pig. "I'll be right back. Left something outside!"*

*He stepped back, holding himself between the legs and hobbling out the door, leaving me confused. I wondered what he could have forgotten outside.*

Does he think he needs a condom? At my age? I can't get pregnant! Or maybe he thinks I'm a whatever my grandkids called it ... a thot—that ho over there. Aha! It's Viagra. It has to be Viagra.

*"Sorry. Back," he huffed, shutting and locking the door behind him. "Care if I stay the night then? Since it looks like we'll be busy all night. Or at least for eight minutes."*

*"My crib is your crib. At least tonight. Then, you'd better get your old, crusty ass out by morning." I smirked, shuffling my feet down the hall and motioning for him to follow.*

*"Deal. But I need to take that dessert with me, too, seeing as though I missed out on it," he said, following behind me into my room.*

*"Oh, you're about to get that dessert, baby." I turned off the Tiffany lamp on my nightstand and stood beside my bed, pulling him toward me.*

*"How can I see anything when you turned out all the lights?"*

"What do you need to see? You want to check if I have meat curtains or something? Well, I'll tell you, I don't. This fine piece of dark meat just likes it not so bright in here, is all. It's like wearing a blindfold. Ever done that, Clyde?" I fumbled with the buttons on my dress.

"Nope. But I'm up for anything. Are you undressing? I can't see," he said.

I heard his pants fall to the floor.

"I'm having trouble," I stammered.

My hands began to tremble, and the arthritis in my knuckles flared. I shut my eyes and tried to gather the courage to admit that I couldn't get myself undressed. Klara had helped me put my dress on, but I hadn't even thought about taking it off. This was just another reason I couldn't get involved with anyone. It was too much mental stress on my part. The shame of baring my frail body and mind wasn't sexy at all. I was a total shit-talker until it came right down to it.

"Do you want to stop?" he asked, reaching out and running his palm down the length of my arm.

"We haven't even started! I didn't mean I'm having trouble with that. I just can't—well, damn it to hell! I can't unbutton these buttons. My hands … sometimes, they don't work right. I just …" My voice faltered. Here I was, Marilyn May, the ferocious sex kitten about to devour her prey, and I couldn't even slip my dress off.

"Shh. I got this. Let me."

Clyde pressed his lips to mine, missing and kissing my chin. Again, I was glad I didn't have those scraggly whiskers. I took his face in my hands and tipped his lips up and into mine. He continued kissing me while slowly unbuttoning my dress and letting it drop to my feet.

I let out a long sigh, realizing that was the most intimate thing I'd ever had a man do for me. Getting old wasn't easy. I had parts that had failed to work correctly for over a decade now.

Clyde kissed the nape of my neck, my shoulders, and my tiny boobs. I had always been self-conscious about my A cups, but the older I got, the more I thanked the good Lord for the pinballs on my chest. They never sagged like the blessed-chest women—like Gloria. I blew out a breath through my nose, thinking of the way she'd looked at Clyde.

*"I'm ready. Let's get to grooving, baby. Let me just get this one last thing."* I sat down, opening the nightstand drawer and searching out the lube. I clasped the old bottle in my hand and hoped it still worked after the last time I'd needed it years ago with Brother Anthony.

*"If it's a condom, I'm clean. As I said, it's been a while for me."*

*"No, it's not a damn rubber. I know your old ass isn't getting laid. Neither is mine. Plus, if we got a disease, we would definitely be in an early grave. It's lube,"* I muttered.

Clyde sat on the edge of the bed next to me, rubbing his palm up and down my spine. I kissed him on the cheek and crawled into the middle of the bed. Still clutching the lube, I held it over my lady cave and squirted out half the bottle.

*"Another one of those old-age things,"* I joked, thankful that he couldn't see my legs splayed in the air while I squirted myself into a slippery mess.

*"It's all right. I'll admit, I took Viagra. I didn't think I needed one, but just in case, I took one. So, no worries about our worn-out bodies. You are as beautiful as the first day I saw you, and no matter how much time has passed between us, I'm going to take you now like I wanted to take you back then against those lockers,"* he growled, crawling on top of me and sliding his meat stick between my throbbing lips.

My old crotch was no longer a raisin or a prune. It had swelled to the size of a plum—ripe and ready to be devoured. When he stuck it in, it was like putting a key in the ignition. I turned on.

*"Thanks for telling me the truth about the dick pills,"* I whispered, taking a deep breath. I couldn't believe this was happening. *"I don't mind. But who said anything about being worn out? I'm revved and ready. But you'll be worn out as soon as I'm done with you."* I wrapped my legs around him and pushed myself up, flipping him onto his back so that I straddled his lap.

*"I wouldn't expect anything less from you,"* he said, clutching on to me for dear life.

I reached across the bed, pinching Clyde's nose whistle to wake him up. The sun filtered through the blinds, which meant he had to go. Klara would be over this morning for her Tinder research, and I'd have to tell her that I'd failed miserably and settled on the first man I had come across.

"What? Where? Who?" Clyde sat up in bed, wincing and rubbing his belly. "Sore abs. Why are my abs sore?" He looked over at me, tilting his head.

"Because you clenched them with each thrust. I know; I felt my hands on them. Can't believe you are as old as you are and still have abs." I pushed myself up off the bed three times before I was able to get up.

"Oh. I still do my morning exercises and stay active when I can. I can say the same for you. Where did you get that energy from last night?" He rubbed his eyes, watching my naked, sagging body walk to the dresser drawer and pull out my purple cotton robe.

"I've had it all pent up for years. I unleashed it on you." I reached around, rubbing my lower back that ached with each step I took.

My thighs felt like Jell-O, and a deep pounding came from between my legs. It wasn't a sexy pulse but a soreness that I hadn't ever felt before. Clyde was much bigger than I'd imagined. He was hung like a horse—or a Clydesdale.

"I'm glad you did." He winced again, groaning with each move he made until he stood, swaying beside the bed. "Phew. You wore me out, woman! Look at me. I'm a trembling mess!" He dragged his feet across the floor, crying out when he bent over to pick his slacks up.

"I told you. I don't mean to rush you out either, but Klara is coming back over, and she is an early morning runner, so she usually stops here after exercising. I don't feel like explaining things," I lied. I was going to brag about how I still had it after all these years.

"It's all right. Look, Marilyn, there's something I need to tell you." He sat back down on the edge of the bed and slipped his legs into his pants.

I tied my robe on and stopped in my tracks.

*Here we go again.*

When I'd heard those words in the past, things usually ended quickly. I knew Clyde wasn't married. I had seen his wife's obituary years ago in the paper.

*He's dying! Lawd, he could have collapsed on top of me in the middle of all that hot lovin' and killed us both!*

"Go on," I muttered, putting my hands on my hips.

"I can't drive. I have to call for a driver. It might be a minute. I'm so sorry. When I went to get something outside last night, I told my driver to go and paid him. I'm old. Real old. I can't even operate a vehicle anymore." He hung his head, refusing to look at me.

I stepped in front of his body and pulled his head into my belly, letting him rest right under my boobs. He had undressed me last night when I was mortified to admit that I'd also lost a part of my independence in my old age. He hadn't even hesitated to unbutton my dress, all the while still desiring me.

"You don't have to be ashamed of that. Ever heard of Uber?"

He pulled his head back and looked up at me. His bushy caterpillar brows drew together as he shook his head.

"It's the service I use sometimes when I don't feel like driving. Too many dumbasses on the roads these days. Get yourself dressed, and I'll make us some coffee. I'll show you on your phone how to use it. No worries, old man." I winked before pulling away and heading toward the kitchen.

The chilled air made the stiffness in my joints almost intolerable in the mornings. I grumbled to Roger and myself as I put a pot of coffee on. We hadn't even discussed my heater and how to fix it, which had been the whole point of our meeting. I had fed and fucked Clyde, and yet my radiator still puttered pathetically in the corner.

I poured two mugs of coffee and set them on the table before Clyde sat down, groaning again.

"Jeez! I feel like I did two hundred squats!" he cried.

I put the sugar and cream down in front of him.

# MAYDAY

"About my heater, we had a deal. I had fun last night, but I was trading you food for work. Not the sex stuff. That was a bonus. Don't you feel how cold it is in here? Look at my nips!" I quickly opened my robe, flashing him my breasts.

"My goodness, woman!" He fanned himself. "It's plenty hot in here to me! But I'll check your radiator before I go. Show me that Uber thing real quick, so I can get that on order before your guest arrives, will ya?" He set his phone on the table, pushing it toward me.

*Knock. Knock. Knock.*

"Too late," I said, digging my heels into the floorboards to push myself up with momentum. "She's here."

"Should I hide?" Clyde scooted his chair back and tried to stand.

"No! What are we, teenagers? I'm a grown woman. I can have men stay the night. Sit your butt down. I got this." I motioned for him to sit before opening the door.

"All right, Ms. May! I want to know all about your Tinder dates. Tell me what you learned during your research! How is love in the geriatric age? Did Clyde or any of the others—" Klara stopped talking when she saw the look of horror in my face. "Is he here? Oh my gosh!" she whispered.

I looked at Clyde, who slumped his shoulders and looked away.

"Klara, I can't talk right now. Can you come back in, like, thirty minutes? Clyde's just leaving. I'm showing him how to Uber." I sighed, knowing that I was going to have to do damage control with Clyde and dish out the details with Klara. I leaned against the side of the doorframe, exhausted already.

"Knotty Pines isn't far from here. Let me take him. I'll tell him about Uber on the way. You sit and have your coffee. You look tired." She winked.

"I'll go," Clyde said, rising to his feet. "I can have someone come look at your heater. I know the best in the business. It doesn't have to be me. Really. I'll go now."

"But don't you want some dessert? I was going to set it out with the coffee." I tried to search his eyes, but they wouldn't meet mine.

"I had a lovely time. No dessert needed. But thank you, Marilyn. For everything." He kissed the top of my head and took his hat off the coatrack.

I opened the door fully, letting him pass me.

"I'll be right back," Klara said, raising her brows. "Let's go, Mr. Clyde! I'll have you home in no time! Meanwhile, pull out that phone of yours and download the Uber app. It's spelled U-B-E-R."

I stood at my entry, watching them pull away and wanting Clyde to look back at me. But he didn't. He kept his face forward, looking straight ahead as if I weren't even there.

I grabbed my coffee cup from the table and lowered myself onto the couch, waiting for Klara to come back and talk. Except now, I didn't feel like bragging anymore. I rubbed my eyes and sighed. I'd hurt him. No doubt, he thought he was being played. Me, Marilyn May, playing a man like I'd been played many times before.

I took a long sip of my coffee and reminisced on that awful feeling of being lied to. That was part of the reason I'd sworn off men for so long. I'd been used by too many scoundrels, and now, here I was, making a good man experience that same terrible feeling. This cold, dead heart of mine was warming up, and just like I had wanted, I felt alive even if my old cooch was turning out to be a heartbreaker.

"I had no idea he was here! I'm so sorry!" said Klara, plopping down on the couch next to me.

"I think we hurt his feelings. I got some explaining to do. He thinks I'm a player. I just know it!" I pulled my robe around me tighter and glanced over at Roger, who still remained unfixed.

"He seemed so sad on the ride home. That must have been it. You broke his heart, gallivanting with all your Tinder dates! Now, tell me about them and about last night." She unfolded the blanket she'd grabbed from across the back of the sofa and threw it over the both of us.

"About the Tinder dates, there's nothing new there. I haven't spoken to anyone else but Clyde since bingo night. And I don't want to after last night. I think I might have taught that old dog some new tricks, and he might have taught me some too." I rubbed the back of my neck in the same spot he had kissed when he flipped me over onto my stomach and went all savage on me.

"Wow, Ms. May! I had no idea. Actually, that's bull. I knew you were a freak. Just hearing you talk about it is … *awkward*."

"What's so awkward? Don't you know I'm still a woman! I still crave that loving touch. Or according to what demon came out of me last night, that raw, fierce, beastly touch. I even let out a roar, and he let out a howl. We were animals. And I thought we'd be going at it again, but I guess at my age, it isn't meant to be anyway."

"Why do you say that? You can find love at any age. Or sex at any age. Whatever you want. What do you want?"

"My damn radiator fixed."

"I don't think that's the whole truth. I've never seen you smile like you're smiling right now. You have the goofiest smirk on your face, like you were up to no good and successful at it. I know you!" she said, curling her knees up to her chin and grinning.

"He helped me with my buttons. I was having a hard time with getting my dress off, and he didn't even bat an eye. He just did it for me. And you know I don't like admitting my weaknesses. But he took care of me. In all the ways." I sighed, fanning myself.

"Wow. That was really sweet of him. Major brownie points! Well, I think he likes you. For him to be a sad puppy like he was on the ride home, you must have made an impression on him. He smiled when talking about you, but I could see the pain in his eyes. He was heartbroken. You'd better tell him the truth. That we were researching Tinder, but you stumbled across him and wanted to do more than this little project with me."

"I will. I will. I am going to need another nap first. We stayed up late. Like, ten o'clock before we both fell asleep!" I rubbed my eyes and situated myself to lay on the other end of the couch.

"I'll let you sleep. Keep me updated on how things go. I'll come back in a few days. Chris had to fly out, so if you want, we can do a barbecue and movie night. I'll pick up some ribs and that slaw you like. If you're talking to Clyde, invite him over again. It will be fun. I won't stay too long, so y'all can get your Netflix-and-chill in. I showed him how to Uber, too, by the way. You're all set." Klara slid out from under the blanket and tucked it under my legs.

"Thanks, Klara. I know I give you shit, but you know I love you and appreciate you. Especially since my children and grandchildren ain't been making much of an effort these days! It was nice, having someone here and being taken care of ... and I did like taking care of him, too, believe it or not."

"But, Ms. May, I thought you said you'd never take care of another man!"

"That's because I never had anyone worth taking care of before." The words slipped out before I could catch them. It was the damn buttons. He had pushed my buttons—the good ones—and he'd undone my buttons. That had sent me over the edge, both physically and emotionally.

"Where is my crotchety old friend, and just what did Clyde do with her?" She laughed, sliding on her shoes and heading out the door.

"That mean old lady is still there. Don't you ever think she's gone. I think I'm just still riding this endorphin high right now." I yawned, pulling the blanket over my chest.

"You enjoy it. Now, get some rest. And when you wake up and can think clearly, call him and explain things. If he's worth it, he will understand."

She locked the door and closed it behind her. I shut my eyes and drifted off into a deep, comfortable sleep.

# *Six*

## CLYDE

*Just one of many for research.* That was what Klara had implied when Marilyn opened the door this morning. I gritted my teeth. Like I was some kind of damn lab rat. Marilyn May had been playing me like a fiddle, and I had danced to her every tune——thrusting my hips this way and that. I couldn't believe I had been so stupid to fall for that trap. I had thought all I wanted was a good meal and someone respectable to warm my bed, but after last night, I realized I wanted more. When Marilyn had spanked my ass and dragged her nails down my back, making me howl, I had known I wouldn't be satisfied any longer as a single man. But it wasn't until she had so easily dismissed my shame about losing my license that I felt something more for her than just a one-night stand.

There was something about losing little pieces of independence when you got to be my age that could send a person into a downward spiral. Today, it was my ability to drive. Tomorrow, it could be my ability to feed myself or wipe my own ass. I was glad to be alive, but growing old was balls—big, hairy, drooping nuts that looked like two ping-pong balls in a pair of tube socks. I'd rather have a root canal, a prostate exam, or even a full-on colonoscopy than to grow old at the rate I was aging.

I flipped the handle on my recliner and put my feet up, groaning. Even my big toe was sore, and I had no idea how. I mindlessly flipped through channels, but my mind was back on last night and just how wild of a ride it had been. I caught myself smiling as I slipped my hand down my pants. The ol' boy could still wake up and stand at attention, even without the Viagra. I felt myself up, gliding my palm up my thick, veined shaft and down into my scratchy platinum man bush. I hoped Marilyn hadn't minded my graying body, but with the lights out, we couldn't see much of each other anyway.

I dozed in my chair, falling asleep before I finished my wank when my phone buzzed beside me. I reached for it, grumbling as I stretched my sore arm out.

*Marilyn: We need to talk.*

*Me: About what? You want to know about old man balls or something for your research? Whatever research that might be.*

My phone rang, startling me fully awake. I cursed myself. I had known better than to get snappy with Marilyn.

"If you want to sass-mouth me, Clyde, you'd better do it on the phone or to my face," Marilyn said as soon as I answered my phone.

"Sorry. I didn't mean to sass-mouth you. Care to explain what Klara was talking about when she showed up this morning? Are you a cake-eater?"

"What? You think I want to have my cake and eat it too? Hell nah. That's what y'all men do! Cake-eaters!" She blew out a breath. "Can't believe you even know what that is."

"Well, I do. I've had plenty of them here, in this old graveyard I live in. If you aren't using me to get what you want, then explain this morning."

"Look, I did plan on doing some research on Tinder for Klara. She's writing about old people and online dating. She said I could meet a man who might be handy around my house while also having some fun and helping her research. I thought, *What the hell?* Then, I took a selfie and jumped into the dating scene for us old farts face-first. But what I didn't intend was to come across an old flame. Or not an old flame, but an old friend. Or someone I'd wanted in my past. That would be you, ya know. You'd left me high and dry back in school, and I really liked you too."

"You wanted me back then?" I sat up in my chair, loudly shutting my footrest. I pushed myself off the recliner and began pacing.

"Of course I did, ya big dummy. You were more than a friend to me. You just never let me know how you felt until you kissed me that day. And then, before I knew it, you were gone and marrying Katherine. I'm sorry about her, by the way. I know we haven't even had much time to discuss our pasts and grandchildren and all."

"It was a long time ago. She was a good woman. But go on. I had no idea you wanted me."

"I did. And I still do. Last night felt good. I'm not going to get sappy or some shit, so don't expect that. But I liked it. I didn't pursue anyone else on Tinder. It was just you."

"But you only reached out to me for research." I paused, leaning against my kitchen counter and rubbing the bridge of my nose.

"I guess. But with the hope of maybe more." She sighed into the phone, and I could hear her foot—or Roger—tapping in the background.

"I had fun last night. But it's going to take me some time to think about all this information. I felt something more for you, and you're a damn tough nut to crack. I have no idea how long I have left. I see my friends checking out of this life left and right. I could die in my sleep tomorrow, or you could. We never know. All I know is that, last night, that thought crossed my mind, and I smiled! I actually smiled, thinking about it. Do you know why? Because if I had died last night, I would have died in your arms, and that would have been a damn fine way to go out." My voice shook as I realized how I probably sounded like I was going senile. Maybe it was the fact that I was aware that, at my age, I only had a few years left, or perhaps it was that I was still riding the endorphin high of banging Marilyn May last night.

"I've never heard anything like that in all my years. I'm truly sorry for any pain I've caused you. It wasn't intentional, and I guess the only choice you have is to believe me or not. I've been in that situation more times than I'd like to admit, and I know how you feel. So, I'm going to give you some time to think about where you want to go in this life and if you want me as a friend or not."

"And what if I want you as more than that? What if I want a second chance at us since I was too much of a pussy back in the day to give it a shot?"

"Well, we'll see. I'm open to discussions on all that. It was nice while you were here. It felt good. All of it. Especially you helping me with my dress. You know that's an embarrassment to me—that I can't always dress myself."

"It's the same way I felt, admitting to my lack of driving skills these days. We were vulnerable. Bared our souls and our wrinkly asses to one another. It was magical for me. But this morning threw me."

"I know. If you want to call me back, call me. If you don't, I understand. We only have a few short years left, if that. Don't waste it, being unhappy."

"I won't. And you don't either." I dragged my feet back to the recliner and gently sat my sore tush into the worn-down cushion.

"I won't either," she said before hanging up the phone.

# MAYDAY

And as soon as she said it, I knew there was no way in hell Marilyn May would let anything or anyone stand in her way of enjoying the rest of her years.

I leaned back in the chair and closed my eyes, contemplating on if I would be happy as a lab rat or if I could be happy as her man.

*Perhaps I can be both.* *YOLO*, I thought as I drifted off into a restless sleep.

Over the next few days, I laid low, contemplating my next move. I hadn't reached out to Marilyn, and she hadn't reached out to me. I wanted to give her space, but at the same time, all I wanted was to cling to her frail body. I wished I could scoop her up in my arms and kiss her on those thin, lined lips of hers. But then, I would probably throw my back out, and that would mean no more nooky for a while.

Even so, I wasn't sure she would want me back in her bed. I never even fulfilled my promise of fixing her radiator. I'd eaten at her place, screwed her sideways, and left in a tizzy. I couldn't blame her either if she didn't want me anymore.

I sighed, switching my TV off and propelling myself off my recliner. My body still ached from my sexcapades with Marilyn, and momentum was the only thing that could get me up out of my seat. I'd even had to roll off my bed and pray to the good Lord that I landed on my feet this morning.

I grumbled, making my way to my refrigerator so that I could look in there, complain about not having anything to eat, and walk down to the cafeteria where they'd tell me it wasn't time for lunch yet. I was just about to lower my saggy bottom into my recliner again when I heard a knock at the door.

"Come in!" I called.

I had no idea who would be coming by at this time unless it was one of my friends from down the hall, wanting me to recount my sexual encounter from the other night. I'd told Cletus and Calvin both several times—and not because their memory was fading. Their memories were fine. They only wanted to live vicariously through my still-working dick.

We'd all been dining at breakfast when the topic of erections came up.

*Calvin said his dick might as well have fallen off. It was useless these days. Cletus told us about a toy he used to help make him hard, which sounded more like a torture device to me. Both Calvin and I were skeptical, but Cletus ran off to fetch it and snuck it back to the dining table under his jacket.*

*"This is my boy, Hoover." Cletus pulled out a long tube. "I got it off that Amazon website. Two days! Can you imagine that? It only took two days to get here! Two days too long for me, but anywho, check it out! It's electric and rechargeable." He pushed a button on the top of the penis pump, and a low hum rang out.*

*"You put your dick in that thing then?" Calvin rubbed himself between his legs, wincing. "Like a cow's udder? Does it suck your stuff out?"*

*"No!" Cletus switched the device off. "It just makes it big and hard. You don't use it to fiddle your diddle! Here, stick your hand in it!"*

*"I'm not putting my hand anywhere near that thing if it's had your saggy, old snake in it! Get that away from me." I made a shooing motion with my hands and pushed my plate of food away from me, suddenly losing my appetite.*

*"I washed it! Actually, that's a lie. Wanda did. She loves this thing. Can't get her off my dick these days because of this bad boy." Cletus patted Hoover and kissed the tip.*

*Both Calvin and I recoiled back in our seats.*

*"You'd be kissing this thing, too, if it solved all your problems. I even use it for blow jobs. Wanda used to be able to take me all the way into her mouth because my junk was as soft as a soggy, wet breadstick.*

*Now, she can't fit me in there unless we do the bed trick." Cletus smirked, tucking Hoover back up under his jacket.*

*"What's the bed trick?" I asked.*

*"You know, when your woman lies at the end of the bed and hangs her head off the edge, upside down. Then, you can hump her mouth, and she won't have a gag reflex. Wanda takes out her teeth when I do it, and let me tell you, I ain't ever felt a sensation like that in my life! Lately, I've had to put a walker behind me and hang on because my knees start to shake, and I don't want to break a hip, fucking my wife's mouth!"*

*I looked from Calvin to Cletus and back again, unsure of how to respond. The mental picture in my head was my best friend's balls slapping against his wife's forehead while her dentures sat, bubbling in a glass beside them.*

*"Where did you swipe the walker from?" Calvin asked.*

*"Really? He just told us one of the most cringeworthy stories I'd ever heard, and that's your question?" I scrunched my eyebrows together, wondering if my friends were losing their minds. It was very possible at our age.*

*"Well, my next question was going to be if he could show me how to order one for myself off that Amazing thing." Calvin held his hand up for Cletus to give him a high five.*

*"It's called Amazon! And they got a lot more than just penis pumps! Let me show you what else I ordered." Cletus rose to his feet and hobbled back out of the cafeteria.*

*I left before he came back.*

My granddaughter Lex walked through the door, carrying two greasy paper bags from one of the local barbecue joints.

"This is a nice surprise! What's the occasion? You want in on my will? Need money for school? Want me to put a hit out on an old boyfriend?" My face lit up.

I didn't get to see my family often. I knew, these days, they were busy with their own lives, and I didn't blame them for not wanting to come anywhere near this stank hole of a retirement community. Knotty Pines wasn't the worst, but it certainly wasn't the best in terms of luxury.

"Grandpa! I don't need a reason. You know I've been busy, but I'll always make time to see you. Thought you might be getting sick of the food around here too," she said, hugging me and setting up the food on my tiny kitchen table.

"I sure appreciate it. This morning, I ate a ground-up waffle. Or at least, I think that was what it was. No lie! They served it with an ice cream scoop. Tasted like maple shit." I shook my head and sat down in front of the plate she'd made me.

"I'm sorry, Gramps. Sounds like prison food." She sat beside me, picked up her barbecue sandwich, and shoved it in her mouth.

"That's what it is. Damn place is a prison. They won't even let me sneak in booze. I had a hot date the other night, and she tried to sneak in some—"

"Wait. Stop. What did you just say? You had a date?" She set her food down and cleaned her hands on a napkin before leaning forward, as if she'd misheard me.

"I had a hot date. That's right; I'm a regular Casanova. Don't you forget it. I'm old, but I'm not dead." I took a bite of my sandwich and grinned. I was probably making my granddaughter cringe just as Cletus had made me cringe with his penis pump.

"Oh gosh. That's just nasty. But go on. What about her? She live here? Is she nice? What's she look like? Do I know her?" Her head bobbed up and down as if she were getting stuck with the tremors too.

Old lady Queenie in room 405 had the shakes so bad in her head that I swore she was a human bobblehead. I wondered how her eyes stayed focused when her head 'bout fell off her neck. So far, that was one thing I hadn't quite gotten around to catching yet.

*But Marilyn … her hands.* I sighed.

"She's beautiful. She's funny. She's kind. Well, kind of. She's nice, but she won't let anyone pull one over on her. Like you. She was before her time, I guess. I've known her since high school."

"How did you meet her again?"

"Tinder."

My granddaughter clutched her heart and dramatically acted like she was falling out of her chair.

*Yep, she'd get along perfectly with Marilyn.*

"What are you doing on a hook-up site?" she cried.

"Looking for a casserole. And maybe some nooky with that cookie." I laughed, slapping my knee. I'd not made a knee-slapper in a while. I would have to remember to tell my friends that one. Though I knew that would never happen. I'd forget it in minutes.

"Okay, this is awkward. So, you met on Tinder. Then, what?" She picked her sandwich back up and began eating, swallowing her food with her repulsion.

I saw the lump in her throat quickly disappear. If this upcoming generation did one thing right, besides online dating, it was how quickly they empathized with everyone around them—including us boomers.

"We were flirty in high school too. It's not like we just met. I've always liked her. She came here for a date once and then made me Sunday supper last night," I said between mouthfuls of meat. Thankfully, my teeth hadn't gone soft like Cletus's dick, and I could still chew.

"Sunday supper is serious! And with a high school sweetheart!"

"Yes, I know. Then, we got super serious after. But ... there was a misunderstanding. She asked me to fix her heater. Then, her friend rushed in and said Marilyn was researching Tinder, and I felt like I was being used."

"And?"

"And? Well, I don't want to be used. At least, I didn't know that I didn't want to be used, but now, I know."

"Are we talking for the cookie, the nooky, or for you to fix her stuff? What was she using you for?"

"Research," I groaned, licking my fingers and wiping them on a napkin.

"For?"

"Her friend's a writer. She is writing about love in the golden years. She wanted Marilyn to research on Tinder. She talked to me about it after we spent a night together. Said she didn't know she would find me."

"So, you're telling me, she likes you. She had intentions of finding a man for play, but instead, she found you. Y'all had a good time, and you're upset because you feel like she tricked you."

"I was upset. I'm not anymore. I know she didn't mean to trick me. I just had a perfect time and didn't expect that. I like her now just as much as I did back then." I glanced toward the nightstand that held my dearly beloved wife's picture, as if she could hear me.

"And you feel some way about her that you ain't felt in years since Grandma left. You're probably struggling with some guilt for feeling the way you do." She wiped her face and balled her napkin in a fist, her gaze not wavering from mine.

*Empathy. I am proud of this generation.*

"I guess you're right. I didn't realize that until I said it out loud. But Marilyn's more than a Tinder hook-up to me. I like her. It all happened so fast. Well, not really since I felt this way back in high school. But still … ya think that's why I'm putting some walls up and hiding out here in this death cell?"

"If she explained herself to you and apologized, then yes. Why wouldn't you chalk it up to a big misunderstanding and go about your business? Do you want to be alone for the rest of your life? You have to get over those fears, Gramps. Grandma wouldn't want you to be alone, and you know it. If you like Marilyn, go get your girl. You didn't stumble across your second-chance romance for nothing."

"How would I do that? I've not talked to her in days. She probably hates me now!" I pressed my forehead into my palms and leaned my elbows on the table.

"You can start by fixing that heater she asked you to fix. Do you need me to take you over there?" Her eyes lit up, sparkling as big and brown as her mother's.

I wondered if she'd call my daughter after this and explain the situation. I was sure she would. Gossip traveled fast in our family. I looked forward to all the phone calls I'd be getting once Lex left.

"No, I can Uber."

She clutched her chest again and threw her head back. "Grandpa, you are too cool. I had no idea you knew about all this stuff."

"You should have seen what I learned about on Amazon!" I laughed, smiling for the first time in days.

I had a plan now, thanks to the smart genes I'd passed down to my grandchild.

Lex and I talked over the next few hours until she had to run to catch up on schoolwork. She told me she'd changed her major for the fourth time, and now, she was studying to become a doctor in the geriatric ward. I guessed I was part of her research too. I congratulated her and let her know how proud I was. She was a ray of sunshine in this slow-moving world I lived in now. I silently prayed that I would see her more often.

I shut the door when she left and hobbled over to my nightstand, pulling the picture of Katherine out and staring at it. I didn't know what to say that she hadn't already heard. I shrugged my shoulders, kissed the photograph, and tucked it back away into the drawer.

# Seven

## MARILYN

"Nope." I swiped left on a photograph of a man standing on top of a dead deer with a rifle in his hand. The deer's mouth hung open at an angle that jarred even my steel soul. I shook my head. "Hell nope."

I continued swiping left through several other men, none of them my type. After about fifty swipes, I wanted to reach out to tell them why they were single. It was something in their pictures—they were ugly—or not in their photos—they were married—or something in their profile—they were assholes. I sighed as I kept swiping for research. I didn't care about any of these men. I only wanted Clyde. But he had long since forgotten about me.

It had been days since we talked on the phone, and I hadn't even so much as received a text. When I checked his Tinder profile, it was gone too. I curled my ragged blanket around me and kept swiping for another few minutes before tossing my phone next to me and giving up altogether.

I stared out the window, shivering and muttering to Roger about how much he sucked.

"If you were a Gladys or a Virginia or any other woman's name, you'd work right. But nope. You are a man, and like all men, you're just a big pain in my ass, Roger," I shouted at my heater from across the room.

I closed my eyes to settle in for my second nap of the day when my phone buzzed rudely beside me. My heart skipped a beat, or I had arrhythmia, but either way, I felt something stirring in there when the hope of Clyde texting me came across my mind. I reached for my phone and saw that it was only Klara.

> *Klara: You doing okay?*
>
> *Me: I was until you woke me up. I had almost dozed off.*
>
> *Klara: Sorry! I just wanted to check on you. Any news from Clyde yet?*
>
> *Me: No. I'll let you know if he ever decides to come around again. I've been swiping this morning for you. Hopefully, I can come across someone and give you some good material. Then, you can finally make me famous in that book of yours.*
>
> *Klara: Deal. But I think Clyde is the one. Maybe you should reach out to him. Don't be a stubborn old bitty. Go for it.*

I would be lying if I said the thought of reaching out to him again hadn't crossed my mind. These last few nights were the loneliest I'd ever had in my life. I hadn't known how sad my evenings were until Clyde.

Back when I had been married, my husband wasn't anything like Clyde. My ex-husband and I didn't have good conversations—or any conversations. He would come home from work, eat dinner at the table, and go work in the garage—or sneak behind there with Gloria probably. I'd never seen them together, but the rumor that floated around on this street was that they'd had a brief fling shortly after I divorced his crusty butt.

My nostrils flared as I remembered the way Gloria had looked at Clyde. I imagined him going over to her house for Sunday supper, and my blood began to boil.

*Oh, hell no.*

I threw the blanket off and pulled from my jealous energy the will to get my old ass up and start baking my crack cookies. If my sincere apology couldn't do it for Clyde, I knew my crack cookies could. Perhaps in person, I could explain the situation better. I'd even make him a non-mushy casserole to go with it.

I shuffled my slippers toward the kitchen, stopping halfway there and realizing that I was doing something I'd said I would never do again. I was taking care of a man. I marched my ass back to the couch and sat back down. This was how it had gone in all my relationships. It was me doing all the work. They were all one-sided. I'd struggled and struggled to do all I could to keep my men, but they'd all ended up being good-for-nothing sons of bitches anyway.

I blew out a breath and lay back down, determined to take my nap. If Clyde wanted my muffin, he'd come and get it. I wasn't about to start the cycle of taking care of a man who didn't want me again. Nope. He would have to fight to keep me, not the other way around. I curled my fists under the blanket, mad at myself, mad at Clyde, mad at the world and all the men who had made me this way.

I rolled over to my side, determined to make myself go to sleep so that, hopefully, I could wake up in a better mood and swipe until I found someone to fix my damn radiator. That was all I really needed—a repairman and perhaps a vibrator. There was no sense in having to put up with anything more.

I shut my eyes tight and relaxed my tense body as much as I could when a knock on my door about sent me rolling off the couch. I wasn't expecting any company today, and usually, my grandchildren and any other visitors called before they showed up.

*Gloria*, I thought.

She was coming to apologize for her catty behavior. She could never stay away from me very long. She didn't have anyone else to gossip to. She'd already run plenty of other neighbors off.

I groaned as I rose from my comfy spot and unlocked my door. My breath caught in my throat as Clyde Jenkins stood before me in ripped-up jeans, a tight white T-shirt, and a tool belt. Yes, a motherfucking tool belt.

"I heard someone was looking to heat this place up." He grabbed his dick and gave it a shake.

"Depends. Can you keep that tool belt on while you work?" I licked my lips, quickly forgetting what I had been pissed about only moments ago.

"Let's find out." He stepped inside and shut the door behind me. "What exactly needs fixing, Ms. May?"

*This dumbass heart of mine.*

"Me. My body. And then my damn radiator." I reached out to tug his tool belt toward me.

"I'm on the job." He smirked, scooping me up into his arms and carrying me to bed.

He tossed me on the bed and pulled out a small rope from his tool belt.

"What the hell is that for?" I asked, eyeing him up and down.

His biceps flexed through his fitted T-shirt with each jerk of his hands as he slipped my pajama bottoms off.

"To tie your ass up. Last time, you got to have your way with me. This time, you're mine." He lightly smacked me with the rope before crawling on top of me and winding it around my hands in a bow.

"You know I can get out of this, right? It's not like it's a sailor's knot." I moved my hands around and slipped one out.

"Damn it. You are naughty, woman! Put that hand back up there," he scolded, tying my hands together tighter.

"Lube," I reminded him, nodding my head toward my nightstand drawer.

"You don't need that with me," he said, licking his fingers before sliding them down between my legs.

He brought his fingers to his lips and licked them again, smiling and moaning before pushing them inside me. I squirmed my hips up, ready as ever for him to pull that hammer of his out and bang me sideways.

"Give me that tool of yours. Let's see what you can fix," I growled, hooking my legs around his ass and pulling him close.

He was still fully dressed, and his tool belt hung heavy on my stomach.

He unzipped his jeans and gripped his cock in his hand, pulling it out. Silver tufts of hair still clung to his droopy balls.

Most of my pubes had fallen out long ago. Yet another thing they didn't tell you about old age. Back in the day, I'd had a bush to be proud of. My bouncy, curly hair down under had been just as styled and pretty as the hair on top of my head. But these days, I was bare, which I hadn't known felt as smooth as it did until Clyde licked his fingers and sent them sliding all over my lady hump.

"Marilyn, I like you. I just want you to know that before I stick it in. Okay?" Clyde cocked his head to the side, dick still in hand, and waited on me to answer.

"You mean to tell me, you're sitting there, about to give me the good loving, and you gotta talk like this? Can't you do dirty talk? Just stick it in and tell me how it feels. Give me one of those *oh fuck*s when you're in there." My legs went limp, and I could feel myself start to dry up.

"No. I really, really like you. This. Us. The chemistry. The fun. The feels. I want you to be mine," he roared those last few words before pushing his thick dangalang so deep inside me that I saw stars behind my half-lidded eyes.

"Unf," I groaned as he bunny-fucked me into the headboard.

This wasn't the pace I'd shown him last time, but I wasn't disappointed in what he was doing. It felt good. He felt good.

"Sliding into you is like sliding into home," he panted, quivering above me. His tool belt scratched me with every quick, deep thrust.

"Come on home then, baby." I latched my legs around him tighter.

I raised my hips to meet his, seeing that look in his eyes. I'd been on this earth long enough to know that look. This man was about to blow his rocket before I even had a chance to get my head in the game. My brain was still stuck on the feels he'd mentioned. I glanced at the clock on the nightstand. It had read 2:38 when he undressed me. It was now 2:44.

"Can't. Stop. Can't. I—Mari—lyn—fuuuuuuuuck." He let out a long breath, diving in and out of me like it was a race before collapsing beside me, breathless. "Did you …" he asked, breathing heavily into my shoulder.

"No. Really? That was less than ten minutes. Did you do anything for me to get there? All I got was my hands tied up and a raw cooter from you moving in and out of me faster than my body could catch up. I think I'm going to have to teach you some stuff, Clyde Jenkins. Now, untie me, so I can at least show you how it's done."

"I'm so sorry. I got carried away. I think the damn tool belt turned me on, and the way your eyes widened when I stuck myself in sent me over the edge. I'll be ready to go in about two hours. Let me get my heart rate down. Maybe a quick nap," he teased.

"Clyde, you know I don't put up with this shit. You came over here in a tool belt and asked what needed fixing. You'd better fix my shit, or I'm taking this rope and tying it around your dick until it turns purple and falls right off."

"Then, I'll keep you tied up." He laughed, kissing my belly and working his way down.

After spending the next two hours in bed, the oxytocin high from our lovemaking sent me back into the kitchen. I whipped up a batch of crack cookies, a casserole, fresh-brewed sweet tea, and biscuits before Clyde came stumbling in from his nap. This time, he'd worn himself out.

"Have a seat." I motioned to the kitchen table.

"No can do. Your new heater will be here any minute. I told my guys to come at five. I got the top-of-the-line heater for you. It's going to be so damn hot in this house that it'll feel like Hades. When you open your front door, Gloria is going to think the devil is stepping out."

"She'd better know it," I huffed. "You bought me a brand-new heater? I thought you were just fixing it. I know those are expensive, Clyde. I'll pay you. You really didn't have to do that."

He sauntered over to me in only the way a man who had scored could saunter—with a wiggle in his hips and a sway in his dick.

"You're worth it," he said, trailing his fingers under my chin and thumbing a scraggly whisker I'd missed.

"Are you tugging at my beard?" I stepped back.

"Is that what that is? I thought it was a crumb or something. Want to borrow my tweezers? I use them for my nose hairs sometimes. I can pluck it for you." He brushed the hair out of my face and tilted my head up to meet my gaze. "Seriously."

"I have tweezers, you old geezer! Sheesh."

"I only meant if your hands weren't able to hold them. I'll gladly pluck your chin hairs for you, Marilyn. And I'll help you with your buttons. I'll fix your lady parts and your broken parts around the house. I'll eat your cookies, smack your ass, and tell you what a damn fine woman you are. I'll warm your bed and soak your dentures, and Lord make it not so, but if I have to, I'll change your diapers one day."

"Now, that's just going too far, Clyde. Too far. I'm not changing any more damn diapers in my life. Not a baby's and not an old man's." I put my hands on my hips and straightened my back, which wasn't an easy thing to do. Lately, I'd been getting that old-lady hunch in my shoulders and slowly shrinking. I didn't know where my height was disappearing off to. Yet again, no one warned you of that either in old age.

"Listen, I know you don't want to take care of another man. But what if you let one take care of you?"

He leaned down and kissed my forehead before prying my hands back off my hips and putting them around his waist, forcing me to hug him. I rested my cheek against that toned chest of his and breathed in the scent of Bengay. Never had I been more turned on in my life.

"As I said, I've got a lot to teach you. But I guess if you're replacing my heater, that's a good start."

I hugged him so tight that my boobs felt like they did when I had to get those damn annual mammograms. Those nurses picked my tits up and put them on top of that metal plate like they were serving a fancy meal before squishing the living daylights out of them. Men never had to deal with that kind of stuff. The worst they got was a finger up the butt and a tug at their balls, which I knew from past experience that most of them enjoyed that anyway.

"Can we at least name your new heater something else? Something instead of Roger? I'm tired of his ass," he groaned, still holding me tight and rubbing my back.

What he had said earlier about me feeling like home was how I was beginning to feel too. Clyde's big man hands wrapped around my frail, old body felt like home. Like I could finally relax.

"Do you have any suggestions on names? Maybe this heater is a woman," I said, not taking my cheek from his pecs.

"No, it's still a man. He's going to be hot and steamy and super reliable. We can call him Clyde."

"Oh, yeah?" I laughed. "Reliable? Hot and steamy I get, but you'll have to show me just how reliable you can be. My track record with relying on men has been zero, zero, and zero."

"I've got this, Marilyn. For the rest of my days and yours. Or as long as you'll have me."

"Put that tool belt back on and get yourself a sip of this sweet tea, and let's get to work then."

"But the men are coming to fix the radiator, not me. They'll be here any moment." He pushed me at arm's length and cocked his head to the side.

"I didn't mean working on Roger, you old fart." I jerked my head toward the back bedroom. "I meant, let's get to work, back in my dungeon." I cracked an invisible whip above my head and winked.

"But the repairmen! They'll be here with your new radiator soon!" He rubbed the back of his neck, looking from the front door to back down the hall to the bedroom.

"Ain't you ever heard of a quickie, Clyde, or is that yet another thing I'm going to have to teach you?" I tugged at his hand, and we both limped our old, achy bodies into the bedroom and back between my sheets.

# Epilogue

## CLYDE

"That pie was the best I've ever had," I said, smacking Marilyn's ass so hard that her buns continued jiggling all the way to the kitchen. I watched her shake it until she disappeared out of sight.

Katherine's picture sat framed on the TV stand, staring at me. Marilyn had insisted we put it on display and give her the respect she deserved. Even I had been shocked at that suggestion.

But lately, Marilyn had softened. But not entirely. She would always be Marilyn May. She'd been a grouchy, old woman all these years probably because she needed to get laid, and I could at least provide her with that. Along with some of my social security check, help around the house, and a secure companionship, heading off into the sunset of life. We didn't have to go alone anymore.

"I know you had a part in this. Getting me out of that old graveyard," I whispered to Katherine's picture. "Thank you for still taking care of me. You were a good woman, the mother of my children, and you'll always have a place in my heart."

I sighed, leaning back in my old recliner that had long since melded to my body, and turned my attention toward the window. Life on Marilyn's street was much more peaceful than back at Knotty Pines. When I had moved in with her a few months ago, I could have sworn I felt my life expectancy increase. I still visited my old friends there now and then, and we'd even rented an Uber for them to come for Sunday supper a few weeks ago. I knew how lonely it could be at our age, and I made an effort to show that I still cared.

Checking into a nursing home or retirement community or whatever the hell label you wanted to put on a damn pre-graveyard situation was one of life's most significant letdowns. Sitting and waiting around to die in an old folks' home was a reality that too many of us, unfortunately, had to endure during our final years.

When Marilyn had suggested that I move in with her and that we could take care of each other, I'd jumped at the chance. I was her hands, and she was my eyes. When I couldn't make out the text in a book, I'd hand it off to her, so she could read to me, and any jars she couldn't open or buttons she couldn't fasten, I'd swoop in like a geriatric superhero. Just call me Super Senior Clyde.

"That pie is the same one I've made the last eight Sundays too!" she called from the kitchen.

"I know, and it keeps getting better. When are you going to make some more of your famous crack cookies?" I yelled as loud as my feeble voice would let me.

She dragged her slippers across the floor and sat down on the couch before answering, "You mean, the cookies I made before I buttered you up to come to be my live-in handyman? You want some more of this crack?" She smirked, rolling to her hip and caressing her butt with her palm while I watched.

I licked my lips. We'd been together for months now, and she still got me going. I'd even thrown out my Viagra because she easily had my blood pumping throughout my entire body. Even the doctor had commented on how healthy—and happy—I'd seemed on my last visit.

"How about you bake some of them cookies, and I nibble the crumbs off that soft skin of yours? I'll turn you over, crumble it over your butt, and get to feasting," I growled, throwing the blankets to the side of the chair and rising to my feet in one long groan.

"Come on over here then and show me what ya got. I thought Klara and Chris would never leave!" She patted the couch cushion next to her.

"You and me both! But I'm glad she's wrapping her project up and that Chris is helping her too. I like the idea he had of putting in my perspective. Maybe women can see how hard we have it now, too, with dating. All them fake profiles, trying to scam me for money. Of course, I always knew a twenty-eight-year-old supermodel wouldn't want to get into my droopy drawers, but I still swiped right anyway." I slowly lowered myself to the couch and let out a sigh of relief. My health was top-notch, but my body was a constant ache from the sex marathon I'd been having lately.

"Clyde Jenkins! You'd better not be swiping nothing anymore, or I'll swipe those droopy drawers right the hell on out of here. You know I don't play that game!" she said, pinching the loose skin on my elbow.

"I deleted Tinder a long time ago! Do you think I can keep up with more than one woman? Especially when I have a woman like you. You're every woman I've ever known, rolled into one. Look at me. I'm worn out just by looking at you. You make my heart race and my knees shake." I dramatically wiggled my knees.

"That's your pacemaker, and you're probably getting arthritis in those knees." She reached across my lap and massaged my kneecaps.

"That's okay. As long as my hips work." I moved her hand to my hard dick and humped her palm.

"You are moaning and groaning, and we ain't even done anything yet. How about we let your body rest tonight? Maybe do something else instead."

"Like what? Watch late-night television and fall asleep on the couch?"

"No. You ain't in Knotty Pines anymore. None of that. We have living to do! Remember that bed trick you told me about? The one Cletus mentioned to you?" She smiled, tugging her dentures back and forth before popping them out into her palm.

"Oh my, woman!" I said, jumping up with newfound energy. "Let's get you to the bedroom!" I pulled her up and onto her feet, dragging her toward the bed. I would have picked her up, except my lower back was catching these days and I was all out of my trusty muscle rub.

"If you teabag my forehead with those saggy balls of yours, we are done though," she mumbled through a toothless grin.

I'd never in my life been so damn attracted to a woman without a tooth in her head as my feisty sex kitten, Marilyn May.

# About the Author

*K*at Addams is a forever twenty-nine-year-old fashionista following her lifelong dream of writing contemporary romance inspired by the exotic men she meets in her worldly travels. At least, that's what she would like for you to think. She's certainly not a stay-at-home mom indulging in excessive daydreaming, frozen pizzas, an unhealthy addiction to purchasing pajamas, and one too many cocktails on the regular. That's some other romance author. The poor thing probably has to sneak away upstairs to write her dirty stories! What would her family think? Thankfully, that's not Kat!

Social Media:

Still crazy about Kat? Rawr! Stalk her on the social media platforms linked below!

> https://linktr.ee/author_kat_addams
>
> (For all of the links in one convenient location!)
>
> Newsletter: https://kataddams.com/free-book
>
> (Bonus *Hotty Toddy* Free E-Book)

Want to keep up with all the mischief and bad decisions? Be sure to subscribe to Kat's newsletter for the latest news. By becoming a subscriber, you'll be the first to know the juicy details on upcoming releases! You'll also be the first to hear of special offers, exclusive content, sneak peeks, terrible ideas, ridiculous shenanigans, and more! As a special gift for signing up, you'll also receive a free e-book, *Hotty Toddy*. Check below for more information on this stand-alone, second-chance, and fake marriage novella.

> Goodreads:
> www.goodreads.com/author/show/
> 19253462.Kat_Addams
>
> Bookbub:
> www.bookbub.com/profile/kat-addams
>
> Amazon:
> http://amazon.com/author/kataddams

DTF: Dirty. Tough. Females.
—Kat Addams's Reader Group:
https://www.facebook.com/groups/
DirtyToughFemales/

(A Facebook group to stay connected, laugh, and share. Hope to see you there!)

Facebook:
www.facebook.com/KatAddamsAuthor

Instagram:
www.instagram.com/authorkataddams

Twitter:
https://twitter.com/KatAddamsAuthor

ARC Team:
https://docs.google.com/forms/u/2/d/
e/1FAIpQLScinoImFEIChW3PQ4_BrlB
oYxpcClYTftNZRz-1DmI-
121R8A/viewform?usp=send_form

(Interested in receiving the latest Kat Addams's books before release? Join the ARC Team.)

# OTHER BOOKS BY KAT ADDAMS

## DIRTY SOUTH SERIES

*Hotty Toddy (Free for newsletter subscribers:*
https://kataddams.com/free-book)

*Grit and Grind*

*Nashvegas Nights*

*Mr. Big Ego*

*Mayday*

## DTF (DIRTY. TOUGH. FEMALE.) SERIES

*On the Rox*